MAKE IT
OUT ALIVE

By

EMMA ELLIS

TABLE OF CONTENT

PREFACE

In her latest book, Emma ELLIS tackles issues such as finding love suddenly, unexpectedly, and through an unlikely source and challenges readers to think about the decisions they would make in similar situations, forcing them to question their own morality. But she does so in a safe space – a fantasy world in the pages of a book. You may not even realize at the time that you are making moral judgments as you are swept along with the story with the pair facing one tragedy after another.

Emma is a writer who loves to travel and is inspired by Paris – the city of love – in her writing. In Make It Out Alive, she introduces us to Violet, a girl who is non-conformist in a way that many of us would like to imagine ourselves to be. Violet is a good person who has rejected some of the ways that society has tried to mold her to its own view of the world. In doing so, she creates for herself a simple life in which her happiness or contentment is judged by her own values. The price she pays for that life is exile from the kingdom and a need to break the law in order to survive. Ryland is the very opposite. An enigmatic character, driven by greed and prepared to ignore his moral compass in the hunt for the bigger buck. As happens to all of us at some points in our own lives, Make It Out Alive throws these two very different characters together and examines how they cope in testing times and alongside a companion who is so very different from them.

The book will appeal to fans of romance novels who also like their stories to be a little bit out there. With

Emma's latest release, you'll find yourself engulfed in dilemmas of the heart while simultaneously having your heart in your mouth as the daring duo battle to find salvation from everything the forest throws at them.

Chapter One

THIEF

Flashes of orange, yellow, and red whipped past Violet as she dashed through the depths of the forest bordering the Kingdom, autumn leaves lining her path of escape. If she wasn't so familiar with her surroundings, she would've mistaken the array of colors for fire.

"She went that way!" A loud shout sounded from behind her, the words echoing throughout the trees.

Violet tightened the straps of her knapsack around her shoulders, a distinct clinking sounding from the handmade sack as it bounced against her back as she ran. The guards seemed to be getting smarter for some reason, able to spot her slipping away from the royal kitchen or the storage rooms of the castle easier than usual. She could usually sneak away with stolen goods and food without a hint of a glance toward her, but it seemed like they were keeping an eye out for her now.

"Got her in my sights!"

A gasp broke from Violet as an arrow zipped past her head and lodged itself in a nearby tree. She prompted herself to move faster, needing to get out of the archer's line of sight before he took her down. They hadn't been lucky enough to do that yet, and she wasn't going to give them the satisfaction. She cut to the left suddenly, veering off of the slightly cleared path that she usually took to get back home when no one was following her. Her knee-high, black boots crunched down on fallen autumn leaves, coaxing the guards her way.

Up ahead, there was an overturned tree, one that she was familiar with. Violet vaulted herself over the trunk before dropping down to crawl and huddle among its large roots. She waited, reaching below her white, long-sleeve shirt to trail her fingers along the black belt fastened around her brown pants. She felt the sturdy handle of her knife, her fingers wrapping around it to slowly draw it out of its holster as she heard the two guards approach her.

"Where did she go?" A burly and stout guard huffed, his red and black armor jostling a little as he came to a stop. He lifted the visor of his helmet to look around better, his eyes narrowing as he scanned the area around the fallen tree.

"I don't know. Are you sure that she went this way?" A lanky archer muttered as he notched an arrow in his bow, wearing lighter armor without a helmet.

"Let's keep going," the larger guard replied before stepping over the tree trunk.

The archer followed, stepping only a few feet from where Violet was hiding in the gnarled tree roots. He heard something faint, like a breath or a crackle of leaves, prompting him to look down.

Before the archer had a chance to get a word out, Violet shot out of the roots, gripping them to propel herself forward. She drove her shoulder against the archer's chest, knocking him back against the bigger guard and sending them both tumbling to the ground. Violet whipped around to run, her foot stepping up on the trunk.

Before she could hop off to run, a sharp pain stung her side, a pained cry breaking from her as she toppled off of the trunk to the ground. The arrow that had pierced her side shot off into the depths of the forest.

"Got her!" The archer grunted as he clumsily pushed himself to his feet. He leapt over the trunk and reached for Violet, grabbing the front of her shirt and trying to yank her closer.

Despite the pain burning through her side, Violet acted on her instincts, throwing her hand with the knife forward to draw the blade against his cheek, blood welling up in the cut. She felt him release her as he cowered back in pain, prompting her to push past her own pain and run as fast as she could back to the original path.

Violet tossed looks over her shoulder continuously, making sure they weren't following her as she ran home. It was a good distance of running, but she couldn't live in the Kingdom. She was close enough to steal things from the Kingdom, but she was also far enough to have some sense of safety. The deeper that she got into the forest, the thicker the brush became. It wasn't only oak trees and berry bushes. There were strange vines and traps with sharp teeth. Luckily, she knew her way around them, knowing which plants and creatures to avoid getting near.

Through the thick of the undergrowth, Violet could see the cabin that she lived in with her grandmother, who had taken care of her since she was a little girl. The cabin was the only home that Violet really knew, and she made every point to hide its existence to also keep Gram safe. She placed her hand over her side, feeling something warm and wet stain her palm as she grimaced. At least she was home and Gram could help.

The cabin wasn't all that big, but it was cozy and warm inside to conflict the cooling autumn weather. Ferns and vines covered the wooden exterior, crawling over the surface and nearly making it blend into the surrounding growth. Two small, square windows bordered the front door, soft light glowing from inside.

Violet stumbled in through the front door, immediately shutting and locking it behind her. She reached and pulled the blinds down over the windows before dropping the knapsack from her shoulders, her teeth gritting in pain.

"I'm back!" She called as she walked through the foyer and kitchen area that were connected to the living room. To the right of the living room was a hallway that led to a few other rooms that made up the cabin. Violet glanced over to see Gram sitting in her rocking chair in front of the fireplace in the living room, flames licking and growling from within the brick arch.

"Oh, what happened now, dear?" Gram sighed worriedly as she peered over her shoulder at Violet. She carefully and slowly pushed herself to her feet, her hand gripping a crafted, wooden staff. She guided herself closer to Violet, her black gown draping across her short figure. Her hair was long and white, flowing down her back like melted snow.

"Archer. I think they're starting to suspect me more," Violet muttered as she slipped off her tactical belt, tossing it onto the circular rug in front of the fireplace. She had to cleanse her knife later anyway.

"You need to put more time between your raids. You're going there too much," Gram told her, gingerly lifting the side of Violet's shirt a little to take a look at the shallow cut below her ribs. She drew in a deep breath before placing her hand over the wound, her eyes closing briefly.

Violet stayed still, feeling warmth flood from Gram's touch, soothing the pain to a bearable level. She knew that Gram had a point, but winter was coming soon. It would be even harder to sneak around and steal things from the Kingdom when the snowfall came. It was hard to not leave footprints in the snow. Plus, food and supplies were scarcer in the winter in general. It was always the hardest season to survive through.

"This will ward off the pain until you can clean it up. I'll show you how to heal it," Gram told Violet as she brought her hand away. She moved to the kitchen to grab a rag, wiping off the blood that tainted her palm.

Violet laughed softly and nodded, prompting a smile from Gram. It was a known joke between them that Violet needed to stay away from magic as much as she could. Early on, Gram tried to teach Violet magic so that she could become a witch like Gram, but things backfired a majority of the time. Violet couldn't even conjure up a simple protection spell around a chair without lighting it on fire. It just wasn't for her, so she turned to combat and sleight of hand.

Some of the plants were feisty, but they weren't venomous or all that dangerous. The tips of their vines were blunt and only slightly bruising, so Violet grew up sparring with them, graduating from hands to knives. She was a terror for the guards of the Kingdom, and none of them had bested her and captured her yet. Some fights were tougher than others, however.

"Or I'll just show you the herbs to use to speed up the healing process and keep it from getting infected," Gram suggested with a little laugh. She started to make some tea, drawing out some canisters of different herbs out of the cabinets in the kitchen.

"Let's do that. I'll get cleaned up," Violet replied before heading into the hallway. She headed to the left and walked into one of the two doors down near the end of the hallway. Her room hadn't changed all that much since she was younger. She had a small bed in the corner, a desk with a few knives that she was working on, a small nightstand, and then a wardrobe for her clothes. There really wasn't much décor besides a rug over the wooden floor and a few magical sigils that were painted on the walls for protection.

Violet kicked off her boots and grabbed a change of clothes from inside her wardrobe, her eyes catching onto a piece of parchment tacked to the inner wall of it. She lightly drifted her fingers along the edge of the paper, a sad smile crossing her face. It was a love letter from her father to her mother, and it was the only thing that she had left of them.

When she was seven, a dragon terrorized the Kingdom, fire overtaking a majority of the houses. One of those houses was her parents', and they burned inside. Violet had been at the local bakery with a few friends, and she had been kept safe in the cellar until the dragon was warded away by the guards. When she returned home, all that she saw was ash and debris. She managed to uncover a few things that weren't burnt beyond repair, and the letter was the only thing that she managed to grab before she was swept away and placed in the orphanage.

Gram must've gotten word about the dragon attack and her being placed in an orphanage because, not a day later, Gram found her playing outside and stole her away from the Kingdom to live with her. Violet was glad that Gram did what she did because the orphanage was a miserable place. At least she was with family again and could mourn with someone as Gram mourned her daughter and son-in-law.

Violet tore her eyes from the love letter, feeling a slight ache in her chest. She hardly read it because it was too painful. Her parents had been so in love, wishing to share infinity with the other. They had a love far more powerful than magic, far more intense than combat. She wondered if she would ever find something like that for herself, but being a rogue was a lonely life. It was just her and Gram, and it would remain that way because she couldn't trust anyone.

After closing the doors to her wardrobe, Violet bundled the clothes against her chest and walked out of her room and into the bathroom. She lit a candle to illuminate the space before undressing. She placed her bloodstained shirt under the tap, letting water run over the stain so that she could somewhat rub away the redness. Most of her shirts looked like that at this point. She pulled on a shirt with the sleeves cut off and another pair of pants that were more flowy and more comfortable.

Violet dabbed at the cut on her side with a damp rag, noting how numb it felt due to Gram's magic. Her magic and knowledge of herbs came in handy quite often, while Violet tried to help out by stealing food and valuables to sell. It was the only way that she knew how to help at this point. She could hold herself in a fight as well if it came to that.

"Doing okay in there, dear?" Gram called from the kitchen.

Violet realized that she had been staring into the mirror for a few moments, the soft blue tint of her eyes seeming dark in the candlelight, which casted an orange glow on the light blonde color of her long hair. She combed her fingers through it, working out various twigs and leaves that had gotten caught in her hair while running.

All of the girls her age, around twenty, in the Kingdom looked so different from her. They wore flowy gowns and had flowers in their untangled, soft hair. They didn't have an ounce of dirt on their skin or any wounds. They lived a life that seemed so perfect, but Violet didn't want it in any way. Despite its danger and risk, Violet liked how she lived. Every day was an adventure, a story to be told. Could the girls in the Kingdom say that about their lives?

However, Violet was aware that the danger element of her life was growing worse. The guards were getting tougher to face. Food and supplies were getting more difficult to steal. She would have to adjust to the curve, or her and Gram would either starve during the winter or be thrown in jail for the remainder of their lives.

Chapter Two

A DASH OF GOLDENROD

The cabin had a secret basement beneath the ground floor that contained anything that Gram needed for her to practice her magic. There were shelves lined with more herbs, but those were rarer. There was a cauldron, a table full of materials, like chalk, candles, a mortar and pestle set, along with other supplies, a built-in fire pit, and a few chairs stacked in the corner. The flooring was concrete, and the roof was enforced so that no one fell through the wooden flooring of the ground floor. The staircase to the basement led up to a secret door in the floor, which was covered by the rug in front of the fireplace.

Violet made her way down a few steps before carefully closing the door above her. She went down the rest of the way to see Gram sitting at the desk, an assortment of different herbs laid out in front of her, along with a cup of steaming hot herbal tea. Violet only came down here when it was extremely necessary. She was afraid that something would catch on fire if she came down here without some sort of supervision.

"What are those?" Violet asked Gram, nodding to a few green stems with tiny, yellow flowers. The herb looked familiar, like she had seen it before, but she couldn't quite place it.

"It's goldenrod. It helps with a lot of things, but one of those things is bleeding. It's anti-inflammatory," Gram explained as she took a knife and started to chop up the stems and flowers. Once everything was finely sliced, she swept the pieces into the mortar bowl before taking the pestle and crushing the herb up.

Violet hummed out of interest, moving to grab one of the wooden chairs stacked in the corner of the room. She picked it up and then placed it near Gram, watching intently as she crushed the herbs into a poultice.

"Goldenrod is a lot like yarrow, which is this white flowering plant," Gram told Violet as she pointed to a bundle of white flowers toward the top of the desk.

"It's better for burns, though," Gram added before motioning for Violet to present her wound.

Violet nodded her understanding before lifting the side of her shirt, the pain of the wound starting to ebb back. It burned like fire, making her grit her teeth a degree as Gram slathered the poultice on the cut. A few drops of the herb's juice drifted down her side as Gram patted the damp herbs against her side.

"Hold on," Gram murmured before reaching forward to grab her staff, using it like a cane to guide herself to her feet. She winced in pain as she shuffled across the hardwood floor in her sandals, her steps appearing painful as she went over to a shelf to grab a small wicker basket. She reached inside to draw out a roll of gauze before shuffling back over to Violet and nearly falling into her seat, a relieved sigh breaking from her as she settled.

Violet frowned as she lifted her arms to let Gram wind the gauze around her side over the poultice to hold it against her wound. She was worried about Gram, who was probably starting to get into her late seventies. She kept getting older and older, and she started showing her age more and more. It was hard for her to move around most of the time, which wore her out. Some days, she would be too tired to do the simplest spells because she felt so drained.

Violet knew that she couldn't slow down time. Even Gram couldn't work a spell like that if it existed. She wished that she could, though, so that she could have more time with Gram, who was all that she had. When she had lost her parents, she had lost everything. Her home had been gone. Her life had turned to ash along with everything else. She had been lost until Gram found her and took her to her actual home.

The amount of gratitude that Violet felt for Gram was immeasurable, and she knew that she would never be able to properly thank her for everything that she did. She just tried to keep Gram as comfortable as possible by having enough food on the table and enough supplies to get them through. When Gram would pass, Violet would be lost all over again, and she didn't know how she would deal with that point in time.

"It'll be good as new in a few days. Goldenrod is powerful stuff," Gram commented, cracking a smile at Violet after securing the end of the gauze down. She turned away from Violet to clean up her desk a little, wiping away any loose herb pieces.

Violet forced a smile onto her face as she nodded, not wanting Gram to worry over her. Violet wanted her to focus on herself and remaining as comfortable and healthy as possible.

"Thank you, Gram. It already feels much better," she replied as she pulled her shirt down. Moments like these really made her afraid of the future when she wouldn't have Gram around helping her.

"Of course, dear. That's what I'm here for," Gram quipped cheerfully.

She was so much more than a medic or a witch to Violet, but she just smiled and turned her head toward the stairs.

"I'm going to go through what I picked up today. I got a few nice necklaces that I can sell," Violet told her as she started to head to the stairs, knowing that Gram would stay behind for another hour or so, like she usually did. She did spiritual work on top of everything, breathing into the world and having it breathe back through her. It was something along those lines. Violet never came around to fully understanding it.

"You should slow down your raids. I'm fearful that they'll find us ... you know what will happen if they do," Gram sighed faintly, her eyes gleaming with worry as she shook her head.

Violet knew where her fear was coming from. Eventually, one day, someone from the Kingdom would accidentally come across their cabin, and it would be over. It was bound to happen, and Violet knew that they needed a backup plan in case that happened so that they knew where to go next. She knew that there were small villages outside of the Kingdom that were safe, but they were a journey, and it would be taxing on Gram. However, Violet knew that she needed a plan regardless. It was better to be prepared than lost once again.

"I'll be more careful," Violet simply said before heading out of the basement. She didn't want to make any promises about stopping what she was doing because she couldn't. They relied on her stealing food, supplies, and things to sell. She couldn't hunt well enough to supply them fully with food from the forest. Besides, she only stole a few things at a time. She tried not to draw so much attention to herself.

Once Violet reached her knapsack that she had discarded in the foyer, she dug around inside to pull out a few apples, a loaf of bread, and a bundle of carrots that she had stolen from a cart outside of the castle. She didn't steal from the poorer class. She only took from those that would be fine without a few morsels of their food. On top of that, she had snatched up a few necklaces from the royal jeweler's shop when the shop owner went to eat lunch. The royal family could spare a necklace or two.

On the road to the Kingdom, there were merchants that she could usually sell valuables to for money or food. She had to be sneaky so that no guards posted saw her, but if she had a hood on, they couldn't tell that it was her at all. Since she had a decent food haul for the day, she figured that she could wait a few days until she went out for another raid. In fact, in a few days would be perfect because the Kingdom would hold its annual autumn festival. With all of the activities going on and all of the people gathered together, it was the perfect cover for her to initiate a good raid.

If she ever wanted a shot at moving elsewhere, she would need money, and the festival would be a goldmine for her if she worked it right. She needed a plan, prompting her to drop her knapsack back onto the floor, the necklaces jingling together within it. She strode to her room, lit a few candles on her desk, and then reached under her bed, yanking out a map of the Kingdom and placing it on her desk.

Most of the time, Violet didn't hide anything from Gram, and it wasn't because Gram could whip up a strong truth spell. She only did it to not worry Gram even more than she already was now. Violet spread out the map across her desk, her eyes moving over the lines that she had drawn on the paper to outline the various buildings and roads within the Kingdom's walls. She didn't want Gram to know about her whole festival scheme because she would be beyond worried.

Violet moved her small, black inkwell closer to her before grabbing her pen, dipping the tip in before marking the center of town. That would be the main area where the festival would be held at. People would make booths to sell goods and food, while performers danced and sang in the very center. The royal family would be seated on a makeshift stage about ten feet away. It would be smart of her to travel on the outskirts of that main area. She could blend into the crowd, but she wouldn't be too close to be spotted.

What she really wanted to do was get into the castle and find the room with all of the gold in it. It was basically a safekeeping room, and it was always guarded by two guards at the door. She had passed the hallway that led to that room a few times when she had been sneaking around, but she had never tried to get into the room before. With most of the guards staying near the royal family down in the center of the Kingdom, the castle as a whole would be less guarded. She could take on a few guards, break into the room, steal as much gold as she could, and then sneak back out to rush home before word got around.

Violet drew a few more lines outlining her planned movements before resting back in her chair, a soft sigh drifting from her. She felt nervous about this because it was a big risk, but the reward was so great. If she pulled this off, she and Gram could pay off a whole stagecoach to transport them to a safer place. It would be sad leaving the cabin, but it just wasn't that safe here anymore. They wouldn't have to live in fear all of the time, but Gram would have to keep her witch business an extreme secret. That had made her a rogue in the first place.

Once a yawn broke from her, Violet rolled up the map and then placed it under her bed so that Gram didn't stumble upon it. She blew out the candles, cloaking the room in darkness as she felt her way to her bed. She laid on her back carefully, being gentle with her wounded side as she pulled the quilted, red blanket up to her chest. She had a few days until the festival happened, which meant that she had a few days left to rest up as much as she could. It would be a hard mission to carry out, but paradise was just on the horizon. She just had to keep reaching for it.

Chapter Three

FESTIVAL
OF GOLD

"I'm going out to pick thimbleberries!" Violet called as she strode to the front door quickly, shifting her knapsack higher up on her shoulders. It appeared empty, but she had a few smaller sacks inside so that she could carry more gold. Today was the day of the autumn festival in the Kingdom, and it would either be a really good day or a really bad day, depending on what happened when she got into the Kingdom.

"Be careful!" Gram called out from her rocking chair. The flames in the fireplace started to die down a little, prompting her to lift her hand. The fire immediately grew more intense, burning a degree hotter.

Violet bid Gram goodbye before shutting the door to the cabin behind her with a heavy breath. It would be safer to turn around and run back inside to hide, but she had a responsibility to the both of them to keep them alive through the seasons, and the hardest one was coming up soon. She strode away from the cabin, stepping through the thick forest and finding her way to the path that had been slightly cleared to lead to the Kingdom. She had walked it so many times that the grass and brush had parted and bent to her many steps and movements. She needed to go through and cover the path so that no one else found it and became suspicious.

With each step closer to the Kingdom that she got, the more nervous that she felt. There were a million different things that could go wrong for one possible good outcome, but it was a risk worth taking to her. Gram probably would have a different opinion, but the decision came down to Violet. She had even brought two knives this time, having worked on wrapping their handles with leather to make them easier to hold. They were concealed under her black long sleeve in their own holsters on her belt over her brown pants. Knowing the outfit would look a bit off for a girl, she had thrown on a black coat with a hood over her clothes. Since it was cold out, no one would bat an eye.

"I can't wait to see the festival! It gets better and better every year!" A child's voice sounded through the trees up ahead.

Violet knew that she was getting close to the road that led into the Kingdom, prompting her to slow down a little bit. She peered over some bushes, watching a mother and a father guide a small girl by her hands toward the entrance. A jolt like lightning crackled through Violet as she watched them swing the little girl, making her laugh and smile. She didn't remember much about her parents, but she knew that they loved her. She remembered the brightness of their smiles and the warmth of their embraces. That was enough for her to know that they cared.

After carefully timing herself, Violet stepped out of the forest and walked onto the road about ten feet behind the family, striding along the dust-covered path naturally. She put her hood up and wrapped her coat around her tighter, acting like she was cold as she headed through the main gates. As she passed by the two guards stationed at the entrance, she kept her eyes down, knowing that it was a bad idea to look at them. That drew attention, which was the last thing that she needed right now.

"Look at the dancer!"

Violet glanced up ahead, seeing a crowd forming in the center area that she had circled on her map back in the cabin. She was in the right area, but she needed to keep her head down. Even from there, she could see the large, wooden stage that had been built for the royal family to sit on and spectate the events. Guards nearly surrounded its base, warding off people who came too close.

Her eyes shifted to the side to see a man a few years older than her standing on the edge of the crowd across from her. He seemed to be glancing at her curiously, his hand shifting to the pocket of his black coat to pull out a piece of paper.

Violet felt uneasy, so she started moving in the opposite direction of him, walking along the outskirts of the crowd in the direction of the castle. Luckily for her, she knew a way to sneak in through the side gate that wasn't guarded. It would just take a bit of a longer walk. She continuously tossed a look over her shoulder, making sure that no one trailed her as she left behind the crowd and weaved through various houses and shops until the castle loomed ahead.

It was grey and gloomy, having multiple towers and stories with long, thin windows. The front door was around twelve feet tall and a dark, wooden style. Guards occupied it at all times, but it wasn't the only entrance. She crossed a small bridge over a deep moat that surrounded the castle on all sides, adding an extra line of defense in case of other kingdoms invading. Luckily, the bridge wasn't guarded unless the Kingdom's alarm bell was sounded, alerting the royal family that trouble was approaching and that the bridge needed to be guarded.

Once she crossed the bridge and approached the gates that also surrounded the castle, Violet walked along the iron gates that bordered the side of the castle before crouching, trying a leg of the iron gate that was loose. She smiled and pushed it up so that there was a gap between the bars that she could slip through. She pulled the leg back down into place before approaching a small side door of the castle. Typically, only servants and guards used it so that they wouldn't have to use the front door. They had no idea that a rogue used it as well.

The first time that Violet had gone into the castle had been a fairly disappointing experience. After hearing so many stories about how luxurious the castle was, it turned out to be the opposite. It was dim and bare inside with cobwebs in the corners. The main halls and bedrooms were kept clean, but the rest of the castle was left to gather spider webs and dust. The royal family's portraits hung everywhere, their beady, black eyes trailing her every move as she crept across the red carpeting down the hallway.

"Start posting these around the Kingdom for everyone to see," a voice sounded from a room up ahead.

Violet glanced around before hurriedly rushing into the room right before that one, cracking the door a degree so that she could watch a guard and a courier walk past her down the hallway. Once they were gone, she slipped out and glanced at the room that they had come from curiously, wondering what they were posting around the Kingdom. It had to be important if it was coming straight from the royal family.

After making sure that the hallway was clear, Violet slipped into the next room, which was full of desks with pens and inkwells and rolling carts. There were papers scattered on the desks and some discarded on the floor. She walked up to one of the desks and glanced down, her jaw nearly dropping open as she stared at a drawing of her. It was a wanted poster with a huge bounty of gold. She was wanted for thievery, of course, but she hadn't expected the bounty to be placed so high. She must've been causing more trouble than she had originally thought.

That meant that she had to move incredibly fast, though. It was bad enough having the guards breathing down her neck, but now all of the townspeople were going to be keeping an eye out for her too because of the large bounty. She rushed out of the room and toward the hallway that led to the safekeeping room, peering around the corner to see the usual two guards there. She pressed her back up against the wall and took a deep breath, calming her heart rate. She was doing this for Gram, for herself.

Violet lifted her shirt and tucked it behind her knives so that they were more accessible. She wrapped her coat around her front, concealing them, before walking out into the hallway toward the guards. She lowered her head a little, peering at them from right under the top of her hood as they gave her a confused look.

"Halt! What is your business here?"

"Show yourself!"

Violet glanced at each guard, noting the taller one and the shorter one. They both had short swords tucked in sheaths attached to their belts. The taller guard would have more reach and would potentially be more dangerous, but the shorter one had more muscle. She weighed her options as she kept striding toward them, her hands slipping beneath the fabric of her coat to grab the handles of her knives on each side of her waist.

"This is your final warning!" The shorter guard huffed out as he wrapped his gloved fingers around the hilt of his sword.

Knowing that she would have a better chance at defeating them before they drew their swords, Violet quickly unsheathed her knives. She lunged forward, raking upward with her left hand to slice the blade up the underside of the taller guard's chin. She buried her other knife in the top right part of the shorter one's chest where his armor didn't cover him.

"Help!" The taller one tried to shout as he grabbed at the cut on his chin, blood welling between his fingertips.

Violet drove her fist against his cheek, knocking him to the ground roughly. She turned to the shorter one, quickly side-stepping a swing by him. She drove her knee up against his stomach, bringing him down to his knees before Violet landed a heavy blow against his temple to make him slump against the ground. They were out, but they wouldn't be for long. She had to move fast. She grabbed the knives before tucking them in her belt.

Glancing between the taller guard and the shorter one, Violet spotted a key ring attached to the belt of the taller one, prompting her to kneel down and snatch it up so that she could unlock the door to the gold room. Once she heard a click, she threw the door open and stepped inside, soft light glimmering in her eyes as she stared at countless gold coins, gold jewelry, gold decorations, and gold-encrusted weapons and clothing that were stacked on tables and rods. It was like a literal gold mine in there.

Hurriedly, Violet yanked off her knapsack and pulled out the two bags that she brought with her. She grabbed at the gold coins first, shoveling them into one of her bags quickly as she kept looking over her shoulder. Heavy breaths puffed from her as she moved fast, not wanting to be cornered in this room. Once one of the bags was full, she used the other to take some of the gold jewelry and decorations, stashing in a gold chalice or two for Gram. She stuffed the two bags into her knapsack, filling the outside with clothing to muffle the clanking and clinking noises.

After checking the outside of the room to make sure that the hallway was clear and that the guards were still knocked out, Violet hauled the knapsack onto her back, adjusting the straps as she carried a larger load. She huffed a bit, straining a little against the weight, but it was doable. She headed out of the room, staggering around the knocked-out guards before making a beeline to the exit.

The Kingdom wasn't all that big, so word got around fast. Once those guards woke up, everything would break loose, and she would really need to hurry up and get out of here and back to the cabin. She gripped the straps in her hands, her knives ready to go in their holsters beneath her coat. She hoped that she wouldn't run into any guards on her way out, but anything was likely to happen at this point. She had actually been able to rob the Kingdom's gold room.

Once she got out of the castle, through her makeshift exit in the gate, and across the bridge over the moat, Violet took to the outskirts of the Kingdom, passing by quiet houses as everyone was out and about enjoying the festival. She could hear the music, cheers, and laughs even from where she was at a few roads away. Some parts of Kingdom life didn't seem all that bad. She wished that she could enjoy the festival like the others, but she was a rogue. It wasn't her plan for her life, but it was who she was, and that wouldn't change here.

"Hey! Not wanting to enjoy the festival?" A male voice called out to her.

Violet glanced over to her left to see the man that was staring at her earlier walking toward her. She felt a chill go down her spine, a sense of trouble filling her as he got closer. He was young with a clean-shaven face, a lean, built body under his coat, white long sleeve shirt and black pants, and short, dark brown hair that almost looked pitch black. He looked too curious for her, so she found herself continuing to walk, trying to get as far away from him as possible. She should've known that something was up when he looked at her strangely earlier.

As she continued walking down the small side street, she heard his footsteps trail her, making her heart pound heavily against her chest. She could hardly breathe as she fought her sense of doom, but she just needed to get as close to the forest as possible. She could lose him there if he continued to follow her. She wondered if he was possibly a guard off duty that recognized her or just some nosy man, but she wasn't about to stop and ask him.

"You're really not going to answer me?" The man chuckled as he trailed her.

His laugh nearly made her shudder, prompting her to speed up her walk. She could hear the crowd get closer up ahead. Maybe she could lose him in the thick of it.

"Violet!"

Violet froze in place, the sound of her name instilling her with pure fear as she slowly turned around to face the man, who was digging something out of his coat.

The man unfolded a piece of paper and held it up for her to see. It didn't take long for her to realize that he was holding the wanted poster of her.

"This is you, right? Wanted for theft?" The man asked her with a little smirk. He wasn't genuinely asking. He was making a point. He had found her.

Even if Violet wanted to answer him with a smart retort or a lie, she couldn't find the words to do. It was like they were trapped in her throat, unwilling to come out. There wasn't much to say anyway. Before she could think about what to possibly do next, he ran straight at her, and Violet had never felt so unprepared and scared in her life.

Chapter Four

RAIN DOWN

Luckily, Violet's instincts kicked in faster than the man's steps, prompting her to whip around and take off. She didn't even care about being sneaky anymore. She just needed to get out of the Kingdom as quickly as possible. She could stand her ground and fight him, but there were too many witnesses nearby, and the guards would be called immediately. She rushed behind the crowd as they cheered for a jester who performed for the royal family, who looked on with bored expressions and sneers.

"Stop!" The man shouted at her as he raced after her, stuffing the wanted poster of her back into his coat pocket.

Violet didn't listen, pushing past people who got in her way with her hands and elbows. She didn't want to be rude and push people, but it could literally be an act of life or death. Her punishment for what she did hadn't been mentioned on the poster, but she was pretty sure that execution wouldn't be a far stretch since the royal family was so greedy about their gold and possessions. Exile would be too kind.

"What's going on?"

"Who is that?"

A whirl of confused voices surrounded Violet as she rushed down the main road to charge through the entrance where she had originally come from. She could hear the heavy breathing and footsteps of the man trailing her, panic and confusion clashing within her all at once. He didn't seem to be a guard, but what was his fascination with her? She supposed that it could be the gold involved, but he was being crazy trying to chase her down like this.

"Alert the guards!"

Violet heard the call from someone, but she wasn't as alarmed as she could be because she was nearly to the forest. That was her domain, her territory. She knew it better than anyone in the Kingdom, and she could use it to her advantage. She hurtled over the bushes that bordered the edge of the forest, hoping that the man would see her going into the thick of the dark forest and just give up.

However, he was ruthless, thrashing right after her through the brush. He had a harder time getting through, but he waved his hands, shoving aside branches and leaves so that he could still see her.

"Violet, make this easy on yourself! Just give up!" The man called out, his voice echoing throughout the forest.

Violet could've laughed at his words. How would subjecting herself to execution be making it easy on herself? She wanted to stay alive, to at least live through her youth, but this random man was trying to bring an end to all of that.

"Never!" She spat back, tossing a glare over her shoulder at him before slipping through a patch of thick trees. The path to the cabin was close by, but he was too near her for her to take it. She had to lead him away. Far away. With a grimace, she headed a bit to the left, veering him in the opposite direction of the cabin and taking him farther into the depths of the forest. The territory up ahead was unfamiliar to her, but she had to keep going. She squinted her eyes a bit as the sun shined against them from up ahead.

"At least give up the gold!" The man tried to reason with her as he dodged around trees and leapt over overgrown roots.

"Make me!" Violet replied, her eyes spotting a patch of thorny vines up ahead. The tips of their thorns weren't venomous, but they hurt a lot when they pierced skin. She saw a small gap between a cluster of vines, her body squeezing itself into a near crouch as she ducked through them. Her teeth gritted in pain when a few caught her cheek and her arms, but the pain was bearable enough to let her stay on her feet and keep going.

The man wasn't as lucky. He wasn't familiar enough with the terrain to know those vines were dangerous. He just saw regular vines, prompting him to plow right through them, their thorns digging into his skin harshly.

"Ow! Seriously!" He snapped as he shook his head, his jaw clenching in pain as he stumbled a little, losing his pacing for a few seconds as he recovered from the sudden pain. He ripped a thorn out of his arm with a grimace before picking up speed, attempting to catch up with her as she dashed around, knowing the territory way better than him, despite her not ever being in this section of the forest before.

Violet could've laughed when she heard the man thrashing in pain behind her. She was glad that Gram had taken her on countless walks when she was young so that she could show her the dangerous plants and the ones that were helpful. Even all of these years later, Violet remembered those lessons. It only took her one time of remembering the hard way for her to secure the information in her mind.

"Might want to watch out for the plants!" She called out to him as she ran into a small clearing with no trees or bushes. There were just fallen, colorful leaves on the ground. She paused for a second, knowing that she needed to lose him soon because she was growing tired. Her chest and throat were starting to burn and ache from drawing in the cold air so rapidly. She decided to go to the right, moving to crouch in a thick patch of bushes with red berries adorning the green leaves. She knelt in the center of the brush, lowering her head and watching the man pause in the middle of the clearing.

A curse broke from him as he glanced every which way, trying to find a clue as to what direction she had gone in. He spun around a few times, shaking his head out of annoyance. Eventually, he chose to go forward, sprinting in that direction and allowing her to finally take in a deep breath to relax and calm herself.

"That was close," Violet whispered to herself as she crawled out of the bushes and laid on the bed of leaves covering the ground. She placed her hand over her heart, feeling its rapid thump as she took a moment to recover. That had been one of the most terrifying chases that she had been in. She supposed what made it worse was him actually calling her by her name. She was so used to "thief" and "rogue" at that point that her name always seemed crueler to call her by for some reason. It seemed more serious, and she still had no idea who he was or what his ties to the royal family happened to be.

Violet slowly sat up and glanced around, her eyes narrowing a degree as she realized that she had no idea where she was at. Feeling her heart rate pick up again, she shoved herself to her feet, looking all around and trying to figure out which direction to head to so that she could get home. She knew that Gram was probably worrying and wondering where she was at now, but she didn't know how to get back to her from here. She had no idea how long she ran for when she verged away from the path, and she had no idea of which general direction that she needed to go in. She was lost.

A soft groan left her as she shook her head, still wanting to remain quiet in case the man decided to double back. Night would be upon her before she knew it, so if she was going to find her way back to the cabin, she needed to do it now. She ventured to the right for a little while, glancing every which way to see if she saw anything familiar, but all of the trees looked the same. It was impossible to figure out where the path was located at in the depths of the forest, especially as it grew darker and darker with each passing minute.

Violet glanced up at the sky through the thick of tree leaves, noting that dusk had arrived. It was becoming nearly too dark to see a few feet in front of her, and she knew that the forest was far more dangerous at night than it was during the day. The nocturnal creatures were typically hunters, and she didn't want to find herself facing off with one of them when she couldn't see anything. She could make a fire and should since it was getting colder, but that would bring a lot of attention to her location. Safety was more important than warmth.

For another twenty minutes, Violet scoured the area for a place to sleep that looked somewhat safe. The limbs of the trees were far too high for her to reach, so she couldn't climb up into the safety of the trees for the night. She probably would've fallen anyway. However, she did find a large tree with its roots sticking out of the ground.

After poking around in the tiny cavern beneath the roots with a stick to make sure nothing was already living in there, she placed her knapsack outside of it and then crawled inside, only able to fit her body.

Violet doubted that any wild animals would be able to drag her knapsack off. She needed to get as comfortable as possible so that she could rest up for tomorrow. The journey ahead would be hard as she tried to find her way back, but at least she had the gold to get her and Gram elsewhere. The Kingdom was threatening to rain down on her, and she needed to take shelter as quickly as possible.

Chapter Five

SNATCHED

Violet found herself up on a hilltop, overlooking a small village that was mostly fields and farms. She could watch the people walk down the few roads that crisscrossed through the village, a sense of peace flooding through her. She actually made it, having fought her way away from the Kingdom to reach a place that didn't want to kill her or Gram. The villagers didn't know everything, but what they didn't know wouldn't hurt them.

Ever since her parents died, Violet felt like she was constantly on the run, but it was like she was running in place or in circles, not actually going anywhere. She couldn't catch a full breath or take a deep rest like she needed to. She always had to keep moving and pitching a look over her shoulder. It was exhausting, but it was better than boring. Now, she was right in the middle. There was hardly any danger, but she didn't feel useless. She still helped Gram and kept her skills sharp. She was still herself, but she was in a peaceful environment finally.

Violet took in a deep breath and smiled, tilting her head up to the blue sky up above, the clouds floating in the reflection of her eyes. She could stay here forever, live out the rest of her life in paradise. No one could find her all the way out here. At least that was what she thought. She hadn't heard the footsteps or the laughing until a hand closed around her wrist, dragging her from the top of the hill. She cried out in shock and protest, a jolt of fear jarring her awake suddenly.

Despite waking up, Violet still felt someone dragging her out from under the canopy of roots. She swung her other hand at the one grabbing her wrist, the moonlight up above illuminating the area good enough for her to make out the man from earlier. How had he found her?

"Let me go!" She snapped, trying to wriggle away as his other hand grabbed her ankle and yanked her out onto the flat ground. She did everything in her power to get away, kicking wildly and swinging her free hand. She felt her blows land at some points, but he seemed to be powering through them.

"Stop … struggling!" The man grunted, releasing her ankle so that he could put his hand up to block his face from her hits. A groan of pain sounded from him as her knuckles caught the side of his head, making his grip on her wrist loosen a degree.

Violet twisted her wrist out of his grasp, yanking herself away so hard that she toppled onto her back with a pained huff, the breath being knocked from her. Despite that, she was prepared for him to approach her, prompting her to kick her right foot forward and strike him in the stomach.

The man folded over, grasping his stomach in pain as he stumbled all the way down to his knees, wheezing sharply. He tried to catch his breath as she pushed herself to her feet.

Violet glanced around for her knapsack, not wanting to leave that behind as she ran from him again. He could take a hit far better than the other guards, making him a force to reckon with and one of the toughest opponents that she had faced. He had far more motivation than the others when it came to catching her. Before she could take another step, she felt a hand wrap around her ankle and pull, bringing her down to one knee awkwardly and painfully.

"Would you stop?" She snapped, trying to wriggle her ankle away from his grip.

"I could ask you the same thing!" The man retorted as he tried to push himself to his feet clumsily. He managed to stand, his hands grabbing at her sides to lift her to her feet.

Violet could sense that she was in real trouble now as his grip on her tightened. She wrestled around in his hold, even trying to throw her head back to strike him. Her heartbeat was so deafening in her head that she couldn't hear anything else. She tried to reach for her knives, but he must've noticed that.

Reacting quickly to the sight of her knives, the man grabbed hold of her better before throwing her against the tree that she had been sleeping under.

The back of Violet's head struck the trunk as she toppled over the roots and down to the forest floor, the leaves crunching beneath her. A pained groan sounded from her as black dots invaded her vision, swimming around in her slightly blurry sight as she stared up at the canopy of leaves above her. She was so stunned from the impact that she couldn't even move for a few seconds, her body remaining limp.

The man took hold of that opportunity and crouched over her, reaching into an inside pocket of his coat to take out a bundle of thin rope. He wrapped it around her wrists, tying them together tightly as she groaned in pain.

"I told you to stop … why didn't you stop?" The man sighed, sounding like he was mostly talking to himself rather than directly to her. He crouched over her, trapping her body between his knees. He drew his hand through his dark hair, taking a breath to relax.

"What is your problem with me? Why are you doing this?" Violet muttered, shutting her eyes tightly for a few seconds as pain thumped through her head. It pounded so heavily that it nearly made her nauseous. What made it worse was that he had bested her this time, successfully catching her. She didn't want to know what would happen to her next, but she at least wanted to know his motivation.

"You're a thief. You need to be brought to justice," the man replied in an almost casual manner, like the words were pre-planned. It didn't sound like a genuine answer that came from his own head.

"Who even are you? You're not a guard," Violet wondered aloud, watching him reach down to pull the knives out of their holsters on her belt. She growled a little under her breath, warning him to be careful with them. She had worked hard on improving them. She wished that she had been able to use them more before ending up in this situation. She never knew being thrown into a tree would lead to her end.

Her words seemed to hit a nerve with him, prompting him to frown and glance away as he tucked her knives into his own belt next to his own knife.

"I'm not … yet. I'm a bounty hunter. My name is Ryland," he introduced himself as he looked down at her, his eyes a glowing green color.

"Well, I would shake your hand, but …," Violet trailed off with a bit of a bite to her tone. She didn't like this situation that she was in. He wasn't being outright mean to her, besides throwing her into a tree and chasing her down, but she didn't trust him at all. He would sell her out, and it was probably because of the gold involved. She hadn't come across many bounty hunters, mainly because it was seen as joke job by those higher up. A person became a bounty hunter when they couldn't make it as a guard.

Ryland smirked a little, giving his head a shake as he took out the poster of her again to look it over.

"Violet … you're worth a lot of gold," Ryland commented, his eyes widening a degree as he investigated the amount, which was into the hundreds. He laughed softly before folding it back up and then tucking it back into the inner pocket of his coat.

Violet figured that he would have the amount of gold memorized. She kept her mouth in a straight line as she glared at him.

"I'm guessing that's why you're doing all of this," she muttered, resting her bound hands against her upper chest. The ropes were digging into her skin a little, but she figured that he would just laugh if she asked him to loosen them a little.

"The gold is the least of my concerns," Ryland chuckled with a shake of his head as he looked up to gaze at her discarded knapsack. He lifted his eyebrows a little at how packed full it looked before glancing back down at her.

"Seems to be the only thing that you're concerned with," he commented.

Violet could've laughed at his words, unable to believe that this guy was actually making a point to judge her. He had no idea what she wanted to do with that gold or what she went through. He was the one intentionally ruining her life for some other strange reason. What in the world could be reason enough to justify what he was doing to her?

"You don't know me," she snapped the words a little at him, any sort of calmness between them disappearing as they held each other's gaze. He already assumed so much about her in the few minutes that they actually talked to each other. If he was going to judge her, she was going to judge him right back. There had to be some leveling of the playing field between them.

"You don't know me," Ryland shot right back, his jaw clenching a little for a few tense seconds. The topic seemed to be a sore spot for him, one that Violet took note of.

Violet huffed and rolled her eyes, breathing in deeply through her nose. She just wanted to make it to the village, to lay in the grass and slow down her life a little bit. She felt like it was going by too fast at this point, and she just wanted to sit back and enjoy at least a little bit of it.

"Good luck bringing me to justice in front of the King. I don't know if you noticed, but we're lost!" Violet quipped, sneering up at him with a smirk. If she couldn't find her way back, he would have an even harder time finding the path back to the Kingdom. The thought nearly made her laugh until she realized that she was still clueless on where to go as well.

"You seem pretty familiar with the forest. Don't you know the way back?" Ryland asked her, seeming a bit caught off guard by her words, like he expected her to show him the way back.

"I've never been this far out. I was just trying to lose you," Violet muttered with a shake of her head, part of her wishing that she had made another decision. Then again, her being lost was better than him finding the cabin and Gram. It was a necessary sacrifice.

"And now we're both lost. Great. Well, we won't get any closer to the Kingdom if we just sit here, right?" Ryland sighed as he stood up, stepping to the side before reaching down to grab her hands. He pulled her to her feet, noting how stiff she came off.

"You might lead us farther away if you take us in the wrong direction," Violet pointed out with a little laugh. It wasn't a laughing matter when it came down to her being stuck in the situation as well, but she would rather both of them fail than him win and bring her to the King. She would rather perish out here in the middle of the forest than be executed in front of the whole Kingdom.

Ryland paused a little at her words, a small frown crossing his lips as he realized her point.

"I don't like being out here," he muttered as he glanced around, looking out of place in the middle of the undergrowth. He scratched at the back of his head, looking a bit creeped out.

Violet smirked at him, rolling her eyes as he glanced around. It was amusing seeing people be out in the forest when they weren't used to the environment. They acted like the forest was the creepiest, strangest place that they had ever seen. To Violet, it was the most beautifully dangerous place that she had ever been in, and she wouldn't change that. The creatures here belonged here, and humans could be here too as long as they didn't disturb the natural order.

"Then you shouldn't have followed me out here. That's what you get," Violet told him, watching him reach forward to grab her bound hands. She dug her heels into the ground, refusing to go anywhere. He had no idea where he was heading to, and he could lead her right into danger, which she would rather not face right now since she was tied up with no knives to protect herself.

"Well, this is what you get for stealing from innocent people," Ryland bit back, leaning forward a little as he loomed over her. He had a few inches of height on her, but that didn't intimidate her in the slightest. He was probably scared of spiderwebs.

"The royal family and its suppliers are not innocent," Violet snapped, hardly believing that he really thought that the royal family was innocent. The King was a harsh and cruel dictator. The Queen was greedy and prideful. The Prince was a brat that demanded that he get everything he wanted. They exploited the poor of the Kingdom, taking gold right out of their pockets before they had a chance to buy food for themselves. It was despicable, and Violet didn't feel an ounce of guilt for stealing from them and providing for Gram.

Ryland nearly scowled and shook his head, gripping the rope tighter as he tried to pull her forward.

"Come on. We can at least find something to eat. If you're nice, maybe I'll give you some," Ryland told her pointedly, his eyes narrowing a degree.

"You can starve," Violet muttered, digging her feet in more and pulling back as much as she could from him. She didn't want to go anywhere with him, especially since he was such a loyalist. He probably didn't care about the gold as much as he cared about kissing the royal family's feet. She didn't understand how people could worship them like that after all of the corruption they brought upon the Kingdom. People were hemorrhaging gold at this point because the royal family wanted so much of it back from their subjects.

"Really now? This is how you're going to be, rogue?" Ryland dealt another low blow with the name. He tried to yank her forward, making her feet slide across the leaves, but she yanked right back with the same might. They were engaged in a vicious tug of war battle with no clear winner.

Violet was determined to not go without a fight. She couldn't use her hands, but her feet weren't tied up. She kicked at his torso, but he dodged around her, side-stepping her vicious kicks.

"That's enough," Ryland grumbled before lunging forward to grab her sides. He tossed her over one of his shoulders, ignoring her cries of protests as she kicked and swung at him. He leaned down to slip her knapsack onto his other shoulder, breathing in deeply through his nose as he balanced the weight on his shoulders.

"Are you serious? Put me down!" Violet shouted at him, wriggling as much as she could, hoping that she would fall off of his shoulder so that she could make a dash in the opposite direction. However, his grip was tight, keeping her completely anchored to him as he started to head to the left after glancing around for a few moments. Violet guessed that he just chose which way to go on a whim, which made her groan. She knew that they were going to get even more lost.

"I will when we find something to eat. I'm starving," Ryland replied as he stepped over more roots and slithering vines on the forest floor.

Violet felt like he would have no idea what would be safe to eat or not. She would have an edge on him in that aspect, but she saw some plants that even she didn't recognize. It was a whole new terrain out here, a territory that Gram hadn't shown her. She would have to rely on her instincts. Hopefully, they wouldn't end up killing her, but it seemed like she would end up in a grave one way or another.

Chapter Six

BERRIES AND VENOM

After ten minutes of struggling on Ryland's shoulder, Violet finally gave in and took a breath, slumping over his shoulder with a defeated sigh. She was beyond frustrated, but she was also really tired after all of that fighting. She just wished that she was back at the cabin with Gram, sitting in front of the warm fire with a cup of tea in her hands. Hunger made her stomach ache painfully, and the cold only got worse and worse.

"Alright, let's take a rest over here," Ryland finally sighed as he entered a small clearing. He carefully bent down to set her down on the ground before dropping the knapsack down beside her as she sat among the leaves. He stretched with a groan, letting his lean muscles recover from carrying her and the heavy knapsack full of gold.

Violet crossed her legs, shivering a little beneath her coat. She was glad for her long hair as it curled around her neck like a makeshift scarf. She sank into the warmth, watching him tighten his black coat around him before glancing at the plants that surrounded them on all sides. They were mostly bushes, some with berries and others with familiar looking vines growing out of their roots. She tilted her head a little, biting into her bottom lip thoughtfully.

"I never learned much about plants ... I probably should've," Ryland muttered as he investigated a cluster of small, red berries. He plucked one of them up and inspected it before turning to her and showing it to her.

"Are these safe to eat?" He asked her, tilting his head curiously.

Violet just stared at him with a faint smile, a casual look adorning her face. She wasn't going to give him an ounce of information. He could taste the berry and try it himself. Of course, it wasn't a poisonous berry. It was just a thimbleberry. However, she wasn't going to tell him that because that sucked the fun out of it, and she would hold on to any ounce of fun that she could have before she was put up on the chopping block.

"Seriously? You can't give me a clue?" Ryland sighed as he rolled the berry around in his hand a few times, weighing the risk. Eventually, he tossed it away with a shake of his head, not wanting to risk being poisoned over breakfast. He looked at the other bushes with a deep breath, placing his hands on the back of his head as his stomach growled.

Violet glanced at one of the bushes with white berries. However, she wasn't interested in the berries. She was interested in the thin vines that grew out of the soil beneath the bush. She wasn't very familiar with the plant, but she knew that the vines were a little aggressive. They were so small though that they wouldn't cause too much harm. They would just distract him while she ran away.

"Alright ... alright. I'm sorry. I'm hungry too. Do you see that bush with the white berries?" Violet told him, nodding to the bush ahead of her. She slipped into her role, feigning innocence when deception was on her mind. She felt a little off about what she was doing, but he was the one bringing her to the King to get killed. She had to fight for herself and for Gram, who needed her and was probably worried sick about her. It saddened her thinking about that, but it only prompted her to continue with her act.

"These?" Ryland asked as he stepped up to the bush, pointing to the white berries.

Violet realized that he wasn't close enough to the bush. The vines were short as well as thin, so he needed to get as close as possible.

"Yeah, could you check and see if they have little, yellow speckles? If they do, then they're safe to eat," Violet made up the lie on the spot. In actuality, she forgot if those berries were safe to eat or not. She watched him lean forward, his feet shifting closer to the base of the bush and the vines as they started to rouse and move around. She knew that they weren't friendly and didn't need much provoking to attack, or at least that was what she had heard about them.

"Um … I don't see any yellow speckles. I don't think so at least," Ryland muttered as he stepped even closer so that he could lean down near the berries. He felt something brush under his pants leg, but he ignored it, chalking it up to nature or the wind softly blowing through the air. He pulled away from the berries, beginning to turn to look at her until he felt a sharp pain in his calf.

"Ouch!" Ryland hissed out, limping away from the bush and looking down at the vines with sharp points that slithered their way back under the bush. A confused and worried look crossed his face as he lowered himself to the ground, hurriedly pulling up his pants leg to reveal a red, irritated sting on his calf, which was already starting to swell.

Violet looked down at his leg and winced, confusion filling her own head at the sight. Typically, vine wounds were just little cuts or even bruises if the tips were blunt. She hadn't seen vine wounds like that before, realization soon dawning on her. That specific vine must've been venomous. She couldn't help but feel cold guilt wash over her, a frown crossing her lips.

Ryland groaned in pain, gripping his leg tightly as pain seeped through it in sharp bursts. He gritted his teeth, closing his eyes hard as he writhed on the ground.

"What's happening?" He gasped out, his leg twitching a bit.

Violet glanced around, her instincts to help kicking in automatically. She felt herself pause briefly, wondering if she should just run. He was injured. This was the perfect opportunity for her to take off and leave him behind. He wanted to bring her to the Kingdom to get killed. Her thoughts clashed heavily between wanting to do the right thing and saving herself.

With a sigh, she pushed herself to her feet and glanced around, looking for any herbs that looked somewhat familiar. She had to cure the venom somehow, and there were a handful of herbs that could do that. She rushed past the bushes to explore the ground, noting some white flowers growing in the browning grass. She recognized these. However, she wasn't exactly sure of what they did. They either helped with venomous effects or they made the person sick.

"Where are you going? Violet!" Ryland's voice sounded through the brush, being followed by another series of painful groans. He fell onto his side, clenching his jaw as a sharp jolt echoed through his leg and throughout the rest of his body. The heat of his skin started to rise, nearly turning fever-ish.

Violet drew in a deep breath, trying to calm the rapid beating of her heart. Gram knew what to do, but she had no clue. She shook her head, feeling herself grow more and more panicked with each second. She needed to relax, but it was hard when someone's life was in her hands. She plucked up a handful of the small flowers before heading back to Ryland, crushing the petals up in her hand. Typically, she would mix this with water or tea to make it easier to get down, but he would have to dry swallow them.

"Here, swallow these," Violet told him as she crouched near him, offering the flowers out to him. Despite the cold temperature, she felt like she was about to break a sweat because she was so nervous.

"What? What are those?" Ryland asked, narrowing his eyes in confusion as he looked at the flowers in her hand.

"I forgot what they're called, but I think they help with venomous plants," Violet explained, her voice coming out more shaky than confident. She really wasn't all that sure about this, but she had to try something to save him. She would never get rid of her guilt if he ended up dying because she had set him up.

"You think?" Ryland questioned her with wide eyes, his head already starting to shake as he shied away from her hand before grimacing.

Violet looked down at his leg, noting how red and swollen it was progressively getting. If they didn't hurry, it would eventually affect his organs. He needed to trust her uncertainty.

"Yes, I think, but you're going to die if you don't do something!" Violet told him with urgency, pushing her hand closer to him again.

Ryland hesitated, a nervous sweat adorning the crown of his head as he glanced between her eyes and the flowers. He grumbled beneath his breath before tilting his head back and letting her shake the crushed flowers out of her hand and into his mouth. He swallowed down the dry petals, screwing his face up at the taste. He waited a few seconds, shaking his head in confusion at her.

"I don't feel any different," he fretted, reaching up to place his hand on his head.

"Well, yeah, it's going to take a few minutes for it to take effect," Violet sighed as she crouched beside him, watching him closely for awhile as he stayed still. She gingerly touched the sting mark on his calf, noting that his skin only felt warm and not hot. The swelling seemed to be on the way down, but it would still take some more hours before his leg was completely healed. These things took time.

"How are you feeling?" Violet asked him slowly, wondering if he was going to be mad or not with her. She supposed that he had every right to be if he realized that she had set him up, but she really hadn't known that the vine was venomous. If she had known that, she would've had him steer clear because she didn't want to be responsible for the death of him.

"Better. I don't feel much pain, and it doesn't feel like I'm running a fever anymore. My leg just feels … tight," Ryland murmured, discomfort sounding in his tone as he awkwardly shifted his slightly swollen leg on the ground. He drew in a relieved sigh, an exhausted look crossing his face as he glanced over at her.

"Thank you … you didn't have to help me," Ryland told her quietly before moving his eyes away, awkward silence filling the space between them.

Violet felt like she didn't really deserve any gratitude from him. She had just been fixing a mistake that she had made. She merely nodded, glancing down at the ground as she moved to sit down a foot away from him. Technically, she could still run, but where would she even go? On top of it all, she was tired and didn't feel like making a mad dash anywhere. He wasn't in any condition to fight, and she didn't feel up to it right now.

"I don't have anything personal against you … I'm just following orders taking you to the King," Ryland voiced to her, rubbing at the back of his neck sheepishly. He still avoided her eyes.

Violet figured that was the case. They had never met each other. Why would he have anything against her? Unless, he was a loyalist that was actually mad at her from stealing from the royal family.

"Well, I'm not stealing gold and food from the royal family just for kicks or selfishness," Violet told him, wanting him to at least know that. Rogues were always seen as selfish, horrible people, but they were just fighting for their lives. She rarely saw rogues in the forest because they didn't want to face off with the environment, taking to the side of the roads outside of the Kingdom instead. What she did see around the forest were bandits, who were far more dangerous than rogues. They took refuge in the forest and preyed on anyone naïve enough to stumble in here. They were lucky that they hadn't ran into any yet.

Ryland lifted his head to meet her eyes before nodding, silence falling between them again for a few moments.

"Do you think we're going to die out here?" Ryland sighed as he glanced around at the environment, which was trying to kill him at every turn it seemed like. He hadn't even spent twenty-four hours here, and he had already almost died.

Violet wasn't sure how to answer that. It was dangerous out here, especially at night. Out in the depths, there were so many things and creatures out here that they weren't aware of that could be preying on them. It would be a different story if they knew where they were going, but they didn't. They were lost with hardly any supplies, no fresh water, and no food available besides berries at that point. On top of it all, the temperature was getting colder. The elements were against them, and as much as part of her wanted to flee from him, she knew that they were safer together.

"I'm not sure yet. I guess we'll see," Violet replied with a little smirk, coaxing one of his own. She sat next to him for a little while, resting and glancing around, wondering if they were even heading in the right direction. She wished that she could have a clue, but all she saw was danger and nature. If they made it out alive, it would be a miracle, and she wasn't a firm believer in those.

Chapter Seven

HELPING
HAND

Since Ryland's leg was still healing, it was pretty clear that they wouldn't be traveling much that day. He moved himself near a tree so that he could lay back against the trunk, his eyes trailing Violet as she wandered around the clearing, carefully studying the bushes.

"I'm surprised you haven't made a run for it yet. I can't exactly chase you," Ryland pointed out as he huddled in his coat, crossing his arms in front of his chest. His pants leg was still rolled up to his knee, the cold air soothing the heat of his skin.

"I wouldn't really know where to go, so there's no point in that," Violet muttered as she started picking some of the thimbleberries, collecting them in the palm of her hand. She figured that they needed to eat something so that they would have some degree of energy and strength in case some other disaster happened. Once she gathered all that she could carry in both hands, she walked back over to him, deciding to share since he was potentially helpless. He would starve or poison himself without her help.

"Here," Violet told him as she dropped one handful of berries into the palm of his hand before sitting down in front of him. He could watch her back, and she could watch his. Even if they weren't on the same side, they had to help each other a degree if they wanted to stay alive long enough to get out of here. She had decided to try to live as long as possible. If there was any chance to get back to Gram, she needed to take it.

Ryland gave Violet a wary look before glancing down at the berries in an unsure manner.

Violet scoffed a little, realizing that he still was iffy about her, despite her just saving his life.

"If you're not going to eat them, I will," Violet muttered before popping a few of her own red, fuzzy berries into her mouth. She chewed on them slowly, savoring their taste, which was a bold mix of tart and sweet. She gave him a pointed look, watching him finally give in and try a berry after watching her eat a few. Her eyes rolled a little as she gazed down at the ground, nudging a few dried leaves with the tip of her black ankle boot.

"Look, I almost died. I'm trying to keep myself kicking," Ryland pointed out with a hard look of his own. He nearly inhaled the berries, eating all of his before she reached the halfway point of hers.

"Bounty hunters don't typically have a long lifetime," Violet commented, cocking an eyebrow at him. Being a bounty hunter was dangerous and exhausting. She had no idea why he would take such a position, especially for a Kingdom that didn't care about him. He was just taking some things off of the guards' list of things to do.

"I won't be a bounty hunter forever," Ryland told her, a slight hopeful tone in his voice as he wiped red smudges of berry juice off of his palm.

"What do you want to be then?" Violet asked him, genuinely curious. No one wanted being a bounty hunter to be their end goal, but it usually was against their will. She didn't know of many that went on to do anything else.

Ryland shrugged a little as he tilted his head back against the trunk of the oak tree.

"I want to be a guard so that I can help people," Ryland murmured, the words coming out a bit faint.

Violet felt like he didn't sound too sure about that, but she didn't comment on that. Being a guard didn't sound like a great position since they were pushed around by the royal family all day. They had to follow the orders given to them or else, and the consequences weren't pretty at all. She didn't know why he would subject himself to being so closely controlled by the royal family.

"There's other ways that you can help people," Violet told him, flashing him a sarcastic smile as he rolled his eyes. Obviously, they had two different views on the topic that they probably wouldn't get over. He could be a teacher or a blacksmith. They helped people in certain ways by providing them things that they needed, like knowledge and sharp weapons. That was all anyone needed to really survive.

"I can't count how many bad people I've brought to justice for their crimes. There are criminals everywhere," Ryland commented as he looked right at her, being bold on purpose just to spite her.

Violet didn't think that someone with such an injured leg should be talking to her so boldly. However, she pushed past her thoughts that told her to kick him in the leg and run. She didn't want to be that bad of a person. She lived her life with the thought that some wrongdoing was okay as long as it was for a good purpose. Stealing to keep her grandmother alive seemed like a good enough reason to erase her guilt.

"You don't know the people that you're taking down. They could be stealing to feed their kids," Violet replied, hoping to make him see the opposite side. He seemed a bit stuck in his ways and in the thoughts forced into his head by the royal family. All wrongdoings were bad. All criminals should be severely punished. Everything was so cut and dry without any sort of exceptions.

"Is that what you're doing? Feeding your kids?" Ryland asked, tilting his head a little curiously.

At first, Violet thought that he was mocking her, but she realized that he was actually wondering if she had kids or not. She supposed that it was a valid question. By their early twenties, plenty of women already had found their husbands and had kids. Since she lived a bit isolated from the rest of society, she hadn't met anyone with a chance of being what her mother had in her father. Maybe she was meant to be all alone.

"No, I don't … I don't have anybody … any kids. I just try to provide for my grandmother as she gets older," Violet murmured as she stuffed her bound hands between her knees, trying to warm them as much as she could since she couldn't stick them in her pockets. She had pondered on having kids a few times before, mainly wanting to gift them the childhood that she hadn't been able to live. She wanted them to live in safety without fearing the world, but she had to get to that same place and state of mind first, which seemed pretty far off. She eyed her knapsack that sat near Ryland, wanting to ensure that it stuck with her through this entire journey.

"It's just you and your grandmother?" Ryland questioned her.

Now, Violet eyed him uneasily. Maybe she said too much. She had just been trying to prove a point that all rogues weren't bad people. According to the law, maybe they did bad things, but it wasn't for bad reasons.

"I'm not going to tell anyone about your grandmother. I was just curious because you didn't mention your parents," Ryland replied innocently enough, putting his hands up in a manner that showed her that he didn't mean her any harm on that front.

Violet found herself believing him for some reason. She nodded faintly before pulling her knees closer to her chest, trying to get comfortable on the hard ground with the leaves under her being the only cushion.

"Yes, it's just me and my grandmother. My parents passed away when I was young," Violet murmured, her eyes drifting back down to the ground. It still stung to say those words. Some days, she forgot that they had died such a violent death, almost believing that it had always only been her and Gram. She craved that blissful ignorance at times because it hurt so badly to remember what reality was actually like. She could've been in the house with them at the time, but she had been spared for some reason.

"I'm sorry to hear that," Ryland murmured, giving her a sympathetic look.

"It's fine," Violet whispered, glancing away from his look. Silence filled the space again, putting some sort of pressure and tension on her shoulders that she didn't like. She didn't talk about deep things all that much. She would talk to Gram every once in awhile, but that became rarer as Violet grew older. She didn't want to worry Gram with the dark thoughts that tainted her mind. She kept them to herself.

"Looks like dusk is coming soon," Ryland commented, nodding up to the darkening sky.

"We should find a place to sleep. Somewhere somewhat safe," Violet sighed as she pushed herself to her feet, glancing every which way for some sort of shelter. Nothing would be perfect, but she wanted a spot where they could be somewhat covered or at least have their backs against so that nothing could sneak up behind them.

"Here, help me up and we'll go look," Ryland told her, extending his hand out to her so that she could haul him to his feet. He tried to put weight on his leg, but he hissed in pain and started to crumble toward the ground.

Violet caught him, motioning for him to toss his arm over her shoulders so that she could hoist him up and keep him from falling. She leaned down a little to let him grab the knapsack and throw it on his outer shoulder before guiding him in the direction that they were originally heading before the whole vine incident.

"Are we looking for another upturned tree?" Ryland asked, a bit of amusement in his tone.

Violet gave him an annoyed look before shaking her head.

"I don't even know how you found me," she muttered as she stepped over a few roots, helping him step over so that he didn't trip and take them both down.

"It was probably because of your snoring," Ryland smirked at her.

"You liar," Violet protested with a glare. She shuffled him to the left, noting a large, dark bush. The leaves were such a dark green that they nearly looked black, and it was so thick that she couldn't even see the base branches within it. It was something that she had never seen before, and she could hear a strange noise coming from it.

"What? What is it?" Ryland asked, his eyes trailing hers toward the bush. He tensed up a little, a sense of unease striking him at the odd-looking plant.

"Maybe we could steal some branches for cover. The leaves are so thick," Violet suggested as he brought him closer toward the bush, hearing a sound that almost seemed to be a low, gravely hum. She let Ryland balance himself out before abandoning his side to get closer to the bush, hearing the hum start to turn more into a deep growl. A confused look crossed her face as the bush suddenly moved, lunging her way as the leaves bent and turned inward, creating something that looked like a row of teeth.

Violet found herself scrambling back, running straight into Ryland's broad chest and sending them both to the ground. She looked back at the bush in horror as it seemed to growl and snap its leafy teeth, thorns now showing. Her mouth dropped open in shock, her focus so attached to the animalistic bush that she forgot that she was laying on top of Ryland, her hands on his chest as she turned her head over her shoulder to look back behind her.

"What in the world is that?" Ryland hissed out, staring at the bush and laying frozen beneath her.

"I have no idea, but I want to get away from it," Violet muttered before turning to look down at him. She felt her face heat up before she hastily climbed off of him and yanked him to his feet, feeling his arm wind over her shoulders. She hadn't meant to topple over him like that. She had just been trying to get away from the snapping bush, which she never expected to ever see in her entire life. The days were growing stranger and stranger.

"I don't like bushes anymore," Ryland muttered as he limped alongside her after grabbing the knapsack, glancing every which way for some sort of space that looked somewhat safe to camp at for the night. He nudged her and pointed to a cluster of three trees growing beside each other. They curved in a little, almost forming a crescent shape.

"How about there? We'd only have to watch one side," he suggested since the trees were curved in enough to cover their back and sides.

Violet nodded, thinking it was a smart idea. Nothing would be incredibly comfortable, but this would be somewhat safe at least. This was another reason why it was best to keep him around until the last minute. If she couldn't tap into his physical help against enemies, she could tap into his mental help regarding shelter and survival. She guided him over to the trees, lowering him down so that he could lean against the right side of the cluster.

"Well, this has been an eventful day," Ryland sighed out, shifting his leg as he leaned his back against the tree, trying to get to a point where he could at least relax a little.

"Expect the same for tomorrow while we're still out here," Violet murmured, glancing around a bit anxiously as the scene darkened. At this point, she was almost too tired to care about any danger. She had faced it all day long, and she just wanted to sleep. She leaned against the left side of the cluster, trying to keep her feet away from his as they rested nearby each other. She pressed her bound hands to her chest, curling up in her coat as she closed her eyes. She could only hope that tomorrow was better. She didn't know how many more rescue attempts and close calls that she had left to spare.

Chapter Eight

EGO

The next morning, Violet marveled at how surprisingly comfortable the tree trunk felt against the side of her head. With her eyes still closed to block out the morning sun, she nestled her cheek against something solid, but it felt smoother than a tree trunk. Her heart gave a little jolt as her eyes flew open, and she jerked her head up off of Ryland's shoulder. She gave him a look of bewilderment when she realized that he was awake.

"Why didn't you wake me?" Violet grumbled, feeling an intense blush grace her cheeks as she leaned away from him. She didn't like how she kept embarrassing herself like this. Maybe it was because she wasn't all that great in a social sense. The only person who she regularly hung out with was her own grandmother, which didn't really count. She didn't know how to act around guys her age, especially ones who were trying to get her killed for trying to survive. She couldn't deny his good looks, but that didn't need to be a factor for anything right now when she was in the midst of the fight for her life.

"I don't know … you were sleeping good," Ryland replied with a sheepish shrug, a faint smirk crossing his lips as she turned away from him quickly. He seemed to catch on to her bashfulness, which made him smile a bit wider.

"Well … I was," Violet muttered before getting to her feet and stretching her bound hands above her head. She heard a soft laugh from him as he got to his feet carefully, putting most of his weight on the tree trunk to test his leg out. She preferred when he acted like this, which was fairly nice. It sometimes made her forget that he was a bounty hunter. She wondered if his sharp and judge-y attitude was just a bounty hunter cover or actually him. There seemed to be more to him than what met her eyes.

"My leg is much better today," Ryland commented as he tested how much weight he could place on it. He slowly walked across the leaves, only hobbling a little bit. The sting wound looked much better and less red, and the swelling was nearly gone. He rolled his pants leg down and grabbed the knapsack, nodding to her that he was ready to go.

Violet swallowed a bit painfully, her throat feeling incredibly dry. She hadn't had a sip of water in a minute, and that would take its toll on them sooner than later. She had no idea where a source of water was located at, but there had to be one somewhere since they were in a forest with thriving wildlife.

"We should find a water source first," Violet suggested, hoping that he wouldn't fight her on this. She knew that he wanted to hurry back and kiss boots, but they wouldn't make it if they didn't get any water soon.

"Yeah, that's a good idea. I'm parched," Ryland agreed with a nod.

Violet blinked at him a few times in surprise, expecting an argument instead of an automatic agreement. However, she was glad that they were at least on the same page for this. They both didn't want to die anytime soon. She decided to head toward the left where the greenery was thicker, figuring a source of water had to be somewhere around the area.

"Don't worry. I'm not going to fight you on everything," Ryland mused, having noticed her look of surprise. He shuffled at her side, putting most of his weight on his good leg.

"What a surprise. You bounty hunters tend to have an ego as big as a castle," Violet smirked, giving her head a shake. He acted fairly differently than other bounty hunters that she had come into contact with, which was a good thing. He was more of a pain to fight since he was better than them, but he was easier to be around in general. It made this whole situation a hint more tolerable since they weren't at each other's throats every second of the day.

"I take it you've dealt with a few before? I mean, you have quite the record. I was trying to track you down for weeks," Ryland admitted to her as they winded through more trees and bushes.

"Weeks? You've been tracking me?" Violet asked him, surprise striking her. She had bounty hunters pop up every once in awhile, but she easily lost them or discouraged them with a fight. They didn't have a long shelf life when they were assigned to take her down.

"They started to notice you a little. Every time that I would try to catch you in the act and take you down, you were already far gone, always a step ahead," Ryland smirked a little, giving her a pointed look. However, it seemed more playful than actually serious, like he was teasing at her.

Violet had noticed the increase in difficulty when stealing. It made sense that they had started to take notice of her, even employing yet another bounty hunter to go after her. He had succeeded in capturing her, but would he succeed in bringing her in? He was good, but she didn't know if he was that good.

"I'm a good planner," Violet pointed out, thinking back on her hand drawn map that she had made just for stealing and sneaking around. She was more prepared than the guards who were assigned to protect such valuables.

"You're a good fighter. That's why they have such a hard time bringing you in," Ryland replied, motioning to her knives that were still attached to his belt.

Violet felt a small smile cross her lips at his words. It was nice hearing them from someone else besides Gram. She enjoyed combat because she felt confidence when engaging in it. It was enjoyable learning new techniques and besting someone trying to bring her down. It gave her a sense of power and control, which were things that she never got to feel in her life, which spiraled so often. Magic was interesting, but she was glad that she had found combat.

"You're not bad yourself. You're the only one who I've had a serious problem with," Violet muttered, cocking an eyebrow at him.

A laugh broke from Ryland as he shrugged, a bold smile playing out across his lips as he glanced at her.

"Did someone teach you?" He asked her.

Violet shook her head, having to teach everything to herself. Gram couldn't exactly help in that aspect besides helping her heal after incidents. She put herself through her own training, keeping herself in shape and teaching herself how to move quickly and efficiently.

"It was just me growing up after my parents passed, so I taught myself," Violet explained before lifting her eyebrows at him, coaxing him to explain his background. She knew that a lot of boys were taught combat growing up, while girls were taught different skills. She went against the fold in that aspect, and she was glad that she did. She didn't want to fall into a mindless pattern like all of the rest.

"That's … really impressive. I was taught by some older boys at the orphanage," Ryland explained, giving her a faint smile before pausing, his eyes narrowing a degree as he glanced around.

"What?" Violet asked, having zoned out while they were talking. She didn't even know how far they had walked. She glanced around, trying to follow his eyes, but she didn't see anything.

"Do you hear that?" Ryland asked her, turning to the left and taking a few steps forward in that direction.

Violet listened more closely, hearing a soft babbling sound from not too far away. Her eyes widened in realization, an excited smile crossing her face.

"That sounds like a river!" She gasped before they both hurried toward the source of the sound, crashing through the bushes and trees until they broke through the edge and a river lay in front of them. It was wide and rapidly flowing, a few rocky edges and discarded branches within its noisy torrent.

Ryland knelt at the edge of the river, leaning down to plunge his head into the water before coming back up with a gasp, his hands smoothing over his drenched hair. Drops of water glided down his face as he tilted his head back, the tip of his tongue drifting along his bottom lip to catch any stray drops. He turned to see Violet staring at him, an amused smile crossing his lips.

"What?" He asked, seeming to snap her out of her daze.

"Nothing," Violet muttered before scooping cool water onto her burning face. She hadn't meant to stare, and she didn't even know why she did in the first place. She just remembered feeling something flutter in her stomach, but that sensation was pretty much gone now thankfully. She cupped her hands again before bringing the edge to her lips, drinking down more water to quench her thirst. It was even more satisfying than the berries.

"Are those fish?" Ryland suddenly asked, pointing to something shiny dashing through the water.

Violet nodded as she looked out toward the middle of the river, seeing a few speckled fish follow the way of the current.

"I think those are trout," Violet told him, but she wasn't one hundred percent sure about that. There wasn't a river near the cabin, but there was a lake. However, the fish in that one were too small to eat. These fish looked like they were a decent size and could be eaten if they could actually catch them.

Ryland suddenly pulled off his coat and stripped off his belt, laying them in a pile near the knapsack as he rolled up his pants legs to his knees. He stepped into the water carefully, looking down at a fish that was slowly drifting through the water.

Violet stifled a laugh as she watched him concentrate, expecting an amusing show. She remained crouched on the edge, her eyes shifting to the fish that he was focused on.

"As a bounty hunter, do you hunt fish as well?" Violet teased at him, a smirk crossing her lips.

Ryland put his finger to his lips slowly, glaring at her out of the corner of his eye before refocusing. He waited a few seconds before jabbing his hand into the water, completely missing the trout and making water splash up against his own face. He grumbled with a shake of his head as Violet laughed, holding her stomach. Ryland splashed water at her with a smirk, watching the droplets rain down on her head.

"Now, that's funny," he chuckled as he climbed out of the river, giving up on his fishing attempt.

Violet wiped some of the droplets off of her face as she watched him sit down beside her on the side of the river.

"Hilarious," Violet mused as she crossed her legs, taking a moment to just admire the river and its coursing blue water. It was dangerous out here, but it was also really beautiful.

"So, how do you know so much about nature?" Ryland asked her curiously, angling his body a little to face her more.

"My grandmother. She knows a lot about herbs and such," Violet explained, not mentioning anything else. She didn't want to delve too much into her own business just in case Ryland sold her out even more. The worst thing that she could do was to endanger Gram.

"It's come in handy. I'm glad she taught you," Ryland chuckled as he pushed his hair back and then rolled up the sleeves of his shirt to his elbows.

Violet glanced at him curiously since he sounded genuine. When it came to him, she felt so confused. They had each other's backs and could joke around in some instances, but they were still enemies. He was still bringing her to the King. However, he wasn't being sharp with her much anymore, and she didn't feel an angry burn in her chest when she was around him anymore.

"Me too," Violet murmured quietly, sharing a brief look with him before ducking her head down and gazing into the water ahead of her. She was afraid of opening up too much around him. It was hard for her to help it because she wasn't used to spending so much time with another person besides Gram. She liked talking to someone around her age and being able to do risky things without having to worry about stressing someone out. She and Ryland dove into risk together.

Ryland parted his lips to say something else to her, but he froze, turning his head to the right to gaze down the river.

Violet followed his gaze, hearing noise down the river as well. She peered around Ryland to see a pair of two bandits coming out of the forest, and they were heading right toward her and Ryland.

Chapter Nine

DOWN
THE RIVER

"Look at what we have here!" One of the bandits with short, brown hair called out to Ryland and Violet. His clothes were nearly rags, draping off of him in tatters. He had a sack that he was carrying that had a few items in it.

The other bandit had shaggy, red hair, wearing the same brown and tan clothing. He chuckled in response to the brown-haired bandit, a few of his teeth missing.

Violet hurriedly got to her feet, her heart pounding heavily in her chest as she watched the bandits come closer. It was too late at this point to run. She should've expected this to happen sooner or later, but she supposed that she had hoped to get lucky. Bandits were aggressive, robbing their way around the outskirts of kingdoms, villages, and anywhere in between. They took advantage of the tired, the desperate, and the lost, and Violet and Ryland were all three.

"We were just about to be on our way," Ryland told the bandits as he stood, lifting his hands to show that he meant no harm. His eyes glanced down at his belt near his feet where the three knives were at, his jaw clenching a little as he looked back up at the bandit.

Violet stepped up to stand behind Ryland's left shoulder, trying to hide her bound hands behind him. She didn't want the bandits to see that she couldn't really fight all that well and try to attack them since they seemed like easy targets. She gazed at them as they stopped about five feet away, noting how dirty they looked. She had learned to avoid them at all costs, and now she was face to face with them.

"Aw, why are you leaving so soon? We haven't seen any other folks in so long!" The brown-haired bandit chuckled, fake pouting as he tilted his head curiously. His eyes landed on Violet's over Ryland's shoulder, a smirk crossing his lips.

"Who have you got hiding behind your shoulder there?" The bandit asked.

"None of your business. We're leaving," Ryland snapped out, taking a step back and coaxing Violet to mirror his step. His eyes narrowed when the bandits stepped forward as well.

"No, you're not. What's in the knapsack?" The redhead growled, nodding to the knapsack near Ryland's feet.

"Clothes and wood," Ryland replied within a beat, locking his jaw tightly as he stared down the bandits.

Violet wanted to step in and help, but she would only entice the bandits to antagonize them even more. She wished that her hands were free because she would've gone ahead and taken care of the bandits by now, sending them back through the woods whimpering in pain. She wasn't going to be bullied around by people like them.

"Really? Clothes and wood? Well, I could use a new shirt. How about you, John? Need a new shirt?" The redhead asked the other bandit with a devilish grin.

"I could use a new shirt, Sam. Why don't you hand over the bag?" John replied to the other bandit before turning to Ryland. The question sounded more like a sharp threat, his eyes zeroing in on the knapsack.

"I'm not going to do that," Ryland replied with a firm shake of his head.

"Then we're going to kill you and take your girlfriend for a prize," John snapped, taking a threatening step forward.

Violet gritted her teeth, heat filling her head as she moved closer to Ryland so that she could whisper discreetly to him.

"We can take them, but I need my hands untied," she hissed to him, wanting to take these bandits down. She knew that they wouldn't stop at any cost to take their things, and she couldn't risk them running off with her gold.

Ryland took a few seconds before subtly nodding. He looked up at the bandits and then down at his belt for a split second before diving forward and grabbing his knife, yanking it from its holster. He quickly turned around and slipped the knife beneath the rope before slicing up, cutting through it in one move. He grabbed his belt and tossed it her way before facing off with the bandits, who rushed forward to stop him.

Violet shook the rope off of her wrists, quickly reaching down to pull her knives out of Ryland's discarded belt. She breathed in deep before running forward, ramming her shoulder into Sam's side to throw him off of Ryland, who was wrestling John to the ground.

"Oh, you're going to pay for that!" Sam snapped at Violet as he hauled his stocky body to his feet. He tried to grab at her, but she side-stepped his hands. He suddenly threw his arm outward, his elbow striking her temple.

Violet stumbled, nearly crumbling to the ground from the sudden blow, but she retained her balance. She lunged out with her right hand, the blade of her knife catching his shoulder as he tried to duck out of the way. She glanced over her shoulder to check on Ryland, who was grappling with John in the grass still.

"Come here!" Sam growled, grabbing at Violet's wrist as blood welled up in the cut on his shoulder. He tried to yank her forward, but she dug her feet in, trying to fight against his attempt. With an angry shout, he grabbed her wrist with his other hand and flung her into the river.

The cold water was a shock to her, lighting up her senses as she swam to break through the surface. She managed to get to her feet, noting how the river got deeper and deeper the farther that it went down. The water gushed against her knees, threatening to topple her over as Sam splashed into the water near her. She had lost her knives in the river, and they were being carried downstream farther and farther away from her. She glanced up when she heard a loud splash, seeing Ryland and John tumble into the river.

Sam grabbed Violet's hair from behind while she was distracted, plunging her head under the surface of the water and holding her there.

Violet held her breath, squeezing her eyes shut as she fought frantically against Sam, trying to break free from his grasp, but it was too strong. She started to run out of breath, her chest aching terribly as her strength started to sap from her viciously flailing her arms at Sam. Her head soon began to feel light, her consciousness starting to slip until her head suddenly broke the surface.

Ryland dealt another punch to Sam's cheek, making the bandit stagger and then fall into the river. He started to reach out for Violet's hand to help her up, but John tackled him into the water.

"Ryland!" Violet cried out as she watched Ryland and John tumble down the river, being swept away too quickly for them to get up. She turned toward the shore, wading through the water before pulling herself out of it. Using the faint amount of oxygen that she had managed to recover, she ran alongside the river as Ryland continued to be swept down it, struggling to keep his head afloat. She noticed that the gushing of the water started to get louder and louder.

Confused, Violet sped up, looking ahead to see that the river dropped off. She stopped at the edge and looked down at the short waterfall, seeing jagged rocks down at the bottom. If Ryland fell, there would be no way for him to survive once he hit the rocks. She had to stop him as he came hurtling down the river, unable to slow his descent down.

Ryland tried to swim against the current, but his body was so sore and tired. It took all of his strength to keep his head above water, some still spilling into his mouth and making him choke painfully. He gasped out, hearing John struggle and cry out downstream from him.

Violet whipped around, trying to hurry up and think. Like with the vine sting, she couldn't mess up. She had to act on her instincts, her eyes shifting toward the forest. She spotted a thin branch on the ground, prompting her to hurriedly grab it and drag it toward the river. She tossed one end into the water, able to reach halfway as she secured her hands around the other end.

"Grab on!" She yelled to Ryland as he started to drift toward it.

John tried to reach for the branch, but he was too far over to secure his hands around it. A frustrated cry left him as he tried to paddle toward it, attempting to fight the stream.

Ryland grabbed hold of the end of the branch, dragging himself along its length as Violet pulled it. Once he tossed his upper body on the shore, a relieved gasp sounded from him, his clothes and hair completely drenched.

Violet tossed the branch away before reaching down to grab hold of under his arms, hauling him all the way onto dry land. She toppled onto her back, feeling him sprawl out over her legs as he caught his breath. She placed her hand on his shoulder as she sat up, her eyes sweeping over him to check him over.

"Are you okay?" She asked him, still feeling her heart pound heavily against her chest. She had been fearful of him tumbling over the edge of the waterfall into the rocks, but at least he was safe now. She couldn't say the same for John as he faced that fate. She wasn't even sure where Sam was at, but she supposed that he had fled.

"I am now," Ryland breathed out, resting his cheek against her knee as he took a few moments to recover from his rough trip down the stream. He groaned as he finally lifted his head, giving her a faint smile.

"Thank you. Again," he told her sincerely as he placed his hands on either side of her legs to prop himself up a little.

Violet felt warmth grace her cheeks as she smiled back, nodding in response. She couldn't let him just die like that.

She felt like she needed to keep him safe, like how he kept her safe. If he hadn't attacked Sam, she would've drowned.

"Thanks for saving me," Violet murmured, moving to wring out her shirt. Her clothes were wet in sort of cool weather, which was not a good pairing. It just made her feel colder.

"Are you cold?" Ryland asked, noting how she tensed up and wrapped her arms around herself. His eyes seemed to narrow a degree, like he was slightly concerned about her.

Violet shrugged a little before eventually nodding. She didn't know what he could do about that, but she was starting to shiver.

"A little. I'll be okay, though," she told him, not wanting him to even ponder on it.

Ryland shook his head before standing up and extending his hand out to her, water droplets dripping off of his skin and clothes.

"No, no. Come on. We should set up somewhere by the river and rest. I think we've had enough for today," he chuckled in a tired manner, his soft eyes prompting her to take his hand.

Violet's eyes shifted from his own eyes to his hand, something stirring in her chest. He actually seemed to care slightly, which was strange. She never expected him to act like this, to show a sliver of concern for her wellbeing. She couldn't deny the fact that she slightly cared as well. She cared enough to not want him to die or get seriously injured. They had saved each other numerous times already.

"Alright, let's go," Violet replied before placing her smaller hand in his bigger one, feeling his fingers wrap around hers. She let him pull her to her feet, his hand lingering on hers as she steadied herself. She guessed that both of them nearly dying was making them so tolerant of each other. There was no other reason for them to be so nice to one another, but she couldn't help but like the new attitude. It made all of this feel more like an exciting adventure rather than her walk to her death.

Chapter Ten

BEARER OF SOULS

Once they took a breath and their hands parted, Violet and Ryland headed back up the river where they were originally at before the bandit attack. They didn't see any sign of Sam, but they did see the sack that the bandits had. They crouched near it, giving each other amused looks.

"Let's see what treasures we find in here," Ryland chuckled as he opened the sack, which was hardly full. He pulled out a few looted items, like silver plates and shiny gems, along with a water flask and two red apples. He tossed her one apple before biting into the other, a soft crunching noise sounding. A pleased sigh drifted from him as he reveled in the taste. He finished it off in under a few minutes, tossing the core toward the forest for some creature to nibble on later.

Violet chewed steadily on her apple as they stood and abandoned the sack, only taking the water flask. The other items probably wouldn't come in handy to help them through the forest, and they had enough valuables in her knapsack. She nudged Ryland after tossing her apple core, nodding and pointing to his discarded knife in the grass. She was upset about losing her own knives, but at least they still had one left in case they needed it, which she was sure that they would eventually.

Ryland bent down and picked up the knife, twirling it in his hand.

The sharp tip of the knife gave Violet an idea, prompting her to gaze up at him.

"Can I borrow that?" Violet asked, believing that she could put it to some use for them.

Ryland gave her a perplexed look, glancing between her and the knife in an unsure manner.

Violet smirked, giving her head a shake as she held her hand out to him.

"I'm not going to attack you. I'm going to try to catch dinner," Violet replied, giving him a pointed look. If she wanted to hurt him, she would have already done it by now.

A look of interest filled Ryland's face as he slowly placed the knife in her hand.

"What are you up to?" Ryland asked her, watching her approach the edge of the river.

"Going fishing. I saw you had matches in your belt. Can you start us a fire?" Violet asked, knowing they would have to cook up whatever she caught, if she could catch anything. She was decent at knife throwing, having used to practice with tree trunks as she got into her teen years.

"Sure," Ryland replied, looking a bit impressed as he strode farther up the river to grab his things. He slipped his belt back on, choosing to leave the coat off for now and drape it over the knapsack. While Violet watched out for any fish, he headed back into the forest to gather an armful of leaves and sticks to build a small fire for them. With his matches, a flame started eating away at the pile in a few moments. He fed the fire as he looked up, watching

Violet slip off her shoes and roll up her pants to step into the river.

Violet finally caught sight of a trout drifting through the stream, her hand with the knife rearing back slowly as her eyes trailed it. She wasn't that familiar with hitting moving targets, but at least the fish was moving fairly slow. She just had to throw a little ahead of where it was going. After drawing in a deep breath and holding it, she tossed the knife at it, watching the blade pierce the trout's body and stick into the riverbed.

"I got it! I actually got it!" Violet cheered immediately, not expecting that outcome. She expected to miss a million times and then give up to go hunt down some berries. She leaned down to grab the tail fin of the trout and then the knife handle, holding them both up. It also felt great to have her hands free finally. Red rings adorned her wrists from the tight grip of the rope, but the soreness was already starting to go away.

"Look at you! Dinner," Ryland laughed out as he tossed a few more leaves and twigs into the fire, which had grown to come up near his knees. He held his hands out for the fish and knife with a small smile.

"Since you caught it, I'll take off the scales and fillet it," Ryland offered.

Violet smiled a little, feeling like that was kind of him to even offer. She handed over the trout and the knife before grabbing her boots and sitting down in front of the fire. She reveled in its warmth as she pulled her boots on and unrolled her pants.

"Thank you, and nice work on the fire," she replied as she watched him take the knife and start to skin the fish, its scales falling and glittering on the ground. She felt her stomach growl painfully, her hand resting over the ache as she watched him work. It was torture having to wait to prepare the fish and then cook it, but it would be worth it in the end to have some energy and nutrients. Being so tired and hungry were really sapping her energy, making it harder to fight and travel in general. Lately, they hadn't been traveling all too much, having to face challenge after challenge, but they were still alive somehow.

"Thanks. I think I cheated, though," Ryland chuckled as he nodded to the pack of matches in his belt.

Violet waved her hand, not caring if he used a shortcut or not. It was better than not having a fire at all and having to battle the cold for another night. Technically, she cheated a little bit by using a knife to catch the fish instead of her hands, but them cheating to survive seemed pretty forgivable. Like she stood by, it was fine to do supposedly bad things for good reasons.

"I'm just glad we have warmth and food. It's tough being out here," Violet sighed, gazing all around as the sun started to make its descent. It felt like everything was against them out here, but it was better that they had each other. She wasn't sure how far they would make it on their own.

"Do you live out in the forest?" Ryland asked her, his tone full of curiosity as he pieced some things together.

Violet shrugged a little, trying to dance around the question and not make him suspicious. It was just still safer to be a bit vague with personal answers.

"Something like that," Violet replied, grabbing a stick to prod at the fire a little.

Ryland carefully drew his knife through the fish to fillet it as he nodded. He put down his knife momentarily to turn to look at her, a small smile quirking up on his lips.

"You don't have to be nervous about telling me about yourself. I wasn't going to tell anyone anything," Ryland told her sincerely, his gaze settling on hers.

Violet held the look, searching his eyes for any sort of dishonesty. It was hard for her to trust anyone when most seemed to be after her. It pained her because she wanted to have friends. She wanted to find a soulmate. She felt like she had missed out on so much normal life that she wished that she could eventually experience. Ryland was a good listener, willing to have conversations with her. It was more than anyone else had granted her.

"I will. Eventually. I just have to look out for myself and Gram as much as possible," Violet explained, hoping that he would understand. In reality, she still didn't really know much about him. She knew that he grew up in an orphanage, which she almost did. She didn't know anything about his parents, his friends, or if he had a partner. She wanted to know more, but she didn't want to pry. She understood that some things were harder to talk about than others.

"Yeah, I get that. I'd do the same thing," Ryland murmured as he stuck one of the fish fillets on a stick and handed it off to Violet. He took the other fillet and stuck it on a stick before holding it up to the fire to cook.

Violet followed his motion, listening to the crackle of the flames. At least he knew where she was coming from. It would be hard to explain to someone who didn't already understand.

"Do you … have anyone that you take care of?" Violet asked, wondering if there was someone like that in his life. He hadn't really mentioned anyone else besides the older boys in the orphanage, who had taught him how to fight, but he hadn't assigned any other importance to them.

Ryland cracked a smile at her question and shook his head.

"Nope. Just me. I live in a little house by myself. I don't see my friends from the orphanage much anymore. They have wives and kids, and I don't have either of those," Ryland replied with a little shrug, not seeming too bothered about that.

"Why not?" Violet found herself asking before she could stop herself. Her curiosity took hold, shoving aside her common sense. It just seemed odd that he wouldn't at least have a girlfriend of some sort. When they weren't fighting, he was particularly charming and kind-hearted. She figured that a girl would've taken hold of him by now.

A confused laugh broke from Ryland as he shrugged, turning over his fish so that the other side could get cooked.

"I just haven't found the right girl in the Kingdom yet, I guess. All of the others rush into their marriages to get settled, but I don't want that. I want a soulmate to go on adventures with. I want a life to look forward to," Ryland explained, glancing over at her with a little smile.

Violet was speechless for a few moments, only able to smile back and nod. She understood where he came from because she wanted that for herself as well. She wanted to enjoy her life, and she wanted to share that enjoyment with someone who she actually loved. She wanted a partner out of compassion instead of just convenience. If she was going to spend forever with someone, she wanted to at least like them.

"I see. I hope you're able to find her," Violet told him sincerely, hoping that he found someone that made him happy, like what she hoped for herself. She didn't want to be all alone in her life. The worst part of being out in the forest was the loneliness, which took a toll when she least expected it.

"Well, what about you? Got some prince stashed somewhere?" Ryland asked her, lifting his eyebrows a hint. As she blushed and looked away, he couldn't help but laugh softly, nudging her with his elbow.

Violet wasn't used to talking about such things. She couldn't really find many eligible husbands in the depths of the forest, so she and Gram never brought it up. They did talk about Violet's mother and father, telling stories about how they met and things they did together. They often loved to travel around the outskirts of the Kingdom, exploring lakes and hills. While her father worked as a blacksmith, her mother gardened and read books at home. They played off of each other so well, vowing to take care of each other until the very end. Violet didn't want to imagine their last few moments together.

"Oh, no. I doubt any guys would like me," Violet muttered with a shake of her head. All of the taken girls that she saw around the Kingdom were flowery and pretty, and she felt like she was the opposite of that. She felt like she was too much, too bold, and that would drive guys anyway. She didn't particularly want anyone like that to begin with, but it still stung a degree because she didn't want to change who she was right now. She liked being strong and bold, able to hold her own. She couldn't picture herself any other way.

"Really? Why do you say that?" Ryland wondered as he drew his fish fillet from the fire, gingerly touching the white flesh with his fingertips to test the heat. When he was satisfied, he tore off a bit of meat before popping it in his mouth, a satisfied hum sounding from him.

"I heard that guys don't like tough girls," Violet told him, giving him a curious look and wondering his take on that. She pulled her fish away and started to tear at the meat, finally starting to sate her hunger.

"Some guys, but they aren't guys you want to be with anyway. I would prefer a tough girl actually so that we could go on adventures and have fun," Ryland commented nonchalantly, his eyes drifting down to stare at his fish as he quietly ate.

Violet willed herself to not look too much into his words, but her stomach flipped, and her face burned regardless. It was nice of him to say that, and she guessed that maybe he just told her that to make her feel better. However, it was still nice to hear because she never expected to hear something like that.

"That's … nice. The fish is good," Violet decided to change the subject, noting the tension between them. She didn't want to say anything or do anything embarrassing, so it would be better to just avoid the topic for now.

"It definitely hits the spot," Ryland agreed with an understanding smile. Silence fell upon them, but it felt like a comfortable quietness. They remained sitting next to each other as the sun fell and the moon rose, the fire between them still burning intently.

Chapter Eleven

FOLLOW THE SUN

Despite her neck aching from sleeping on the ground near the river, Violet woke up the next morning feeling fairly content. She was just glad that she had slept well after the craziness of yesterday. She sat up quietly, noticing that Ryland was still asleep near her. It looked like the fire had gone out a few hours ago, leaving burnt leaves and twigs in its wake. She stretched her arms above her head, sighing softly as she glanced out at the river. Its babbling had lulled her to sleep almost immediately after she got done eating and laid down last night.

Now, they had to move forward today, and there was no telling where they were heading to. She wished that she could at least figure out the right direction of where to go because that would eliminate a lot of confusion and uncertainty. She tried to remember anything about that day that they first ran into the forest, her thoughts drifting back to any details. She remembered dodging past thorny bushes and finding it hard to see at certain points because the sun was in her face. Then, it hit her. The sun had been making its descent ahead of her.

Violet stood up, glancing to the left where the sun was rising into the sky. She realized that was the direction back toward the Kingdom since it was the opposite way that she ran, and the sun was facing her before. She could've cheered at her realization, her heart rate soaring. They could finally find their way out of the forest if they went in the rising direction of the sun. She turned and knelt near Ryland, shaking him lightly to wake him up. He needed to know about this.

"Ryland! Wake up!" She whispered, pushing at his shoulder rapidly.

"Hm? What?" Ryland mumbled sleepily, popping one eye open as he lifted his head, giving her a confused look. He saw her wide eyes and sat up quickly, turning his head every which way.

"What is it? Is something happening?" Ryland asked, a hint of panic in his voice as he was jarred from his drowsy state.

Violet placed her hands on his shoulders, grounding him as she met his gaze.

"I know which direction we need to go," she told him, making his eyes widen even more at her words. She pointed to the sun behind her.

"The sun was descending and shining in my face when we ran into the forest, so we need to go the opposite way. We need to head toward where the sun is rising," Violet explained before nodding in the other direction behind him.

Ryland turned his head to gaze in that direction, a look of realization dawning on him as he nodded.

"Of course. We can actually find our way out of here," he laughed a little out of relief, his head tilting back as he drew in a deep breath. Being out in the forest was exhausting, especially when they didn't have many supplies. He shared a smile with her before getting to his feet and grabbing the water canteen that used to belong to the bandits. He knelt near the river and filled the canteen up, already beginning to prepare for their journey back since they had an idea of where to go finally.

Violet glanced over at the cut ropes on the ground a few feet away, hoping that he wouldn't tie her up again. She figured that he had to have some level of trust in her now after everything that they had gone through. She didn't feel safe enough to part from him still, and she wished that she didn't have to. She felt like there was so much potential for friendship for them … maybe something more at a point.

With a shake of her head, Violet rushed her thoughts off, not wanting to think like that and get her hopes up. She had to remember his end goal for her, which wasn't in her best interest. She had to look out for herself and Gram, even if that meant going against him. She ignored the ropes and waited for him to put on his coat and the knapsack, his hand reaching out to hand the water canteen to her.

"Can you carry this?" Ryland asked her as he stopped at her side. Once she nodded and took the canteen, he noticed her eyes shoot down toward the ground to look at something. He followed her gaze to the broken rope on the ground, a soft sigh breaking from him as he turned to look at her.

"I don't think there's much point in that anymore. You would've run off already," Ryland pointed out as he bumped his shoulder against hers, motioning for her to follow him up the river toward the rising sun.

Violet fell into step at his side, smiling silently to herself. Maybe there was hope for him to change his mind about taking her in. Maybe they could salvage what was beginning to grow between them. It would be a problem for another day. For now, she just wanted to fight her way through the forest with him.

"Maybe the King will be light on your sentence and just banish you," Ryland commented, a hint of hopefulness in his voice.

At least he didn't want her to be killed. He still felt like he had to turn her in for some reason that she didn't understand. She shrugged a little, her eyes falling on the knapsack that was on his back.

"My original plan with the gold was to use it to get as far away from the Kingdom as possible. It's not safe for Gram and me around there," Violet told him before chewing on her bottom lip anxiously. She hoped that she could somehow do that. No matter what, the Kingdom would always pose a threat to her and Gram if they remained in their cabin.

"Why are you guys in such danger?" Ryland asked her, slowing his pace a little so that he could glance her way, his eyes narrowing a degree.

Violet paused while walking to pick a few thimbleberries off of a bush, rolling a few around in the palm of her hand before popping them in her mouth. She was hungry, but she also wanted some time to think before answering. She picked a few more berries before handing them over to Ryland and drawing in a deep breath.

"My grandmother is a witch. They banished her awhile ago, but she wanted to stay close to her family, which was my mom and my dad when they were still alive and then me when I was born," Violet revealed, keeping her eyes on the berry bush, too afraid to see his reaction. People typically reacted very adversely to witches, believing that they were evil to their very core. It just wasn't true. Gram was one of the sweetest people who Violet had ever been around, and people would think the same if they just gave her a chance.

"No wonder you know so much about herbs. Can you do any magic?" Ryland asked, sounding more excited and intrigued than angered.

Violet looked up at him out of confusion, not expecting his response.

"I tried to learn, but everything kept backfiring. I can't count how many times I accidentally set something on fire," she said meekly, feeling a bit bashful as he chuckled.

"You can't be good at everything," Ryland teased at her, shooting her a playful wink before leading her back up the river. Up ahead, the river seemed to veer to the right, more forest replacing its path. It looked like they were about to delve right back into the depths of the forest once again without the comfort of the river nearby.

"Hush," Violet smirked, giving him a light shove as she shook her head before speaking once more. There was a lot to say on the topic, words that she hadn't really spoken aloud before. It felt relieving finally speaking them into the world around her, like she was freeing herself in a way that she hadn't been able to before by trapping all of those thoughts in her head.

"People hate witches so much, and I never really fit in around the Kingdom. It's just a painful reminder of what happened to my parents, so that's why I just want to get as far away as I can," Violet sighed, having nothing positive to connect to the Kingdom. It was all hate and fire, and she was tired of constantly getting burned. The fire was already starting to get out of control.

"What happened to your parents? If you don't mind me asking," Ryland asked quietly, his words coming out soft as their arms lightly brushed as they walked.

Violet watched her boots kick through red, orange, and yellow leaves, listening to the crunch and swish. It was easier to disassociate than remember what happened all of those years ago. As time went on, she lost more and more details, and she didn't know whether to be relieved or devastated.

"I was seven and playing with some other kids away from my house. A dragon came down and attacked the Kingdom - I'm sure you remember the attack - and burned down a whole row of houses. One of those houses was mine. My parents were both at home, and I just happened to be in the right place at the right time because I was brought to safety in a bakery. I should've been there with them," Violet breathed out the last part, always wondering if it would've been better if she had gone with her parents so that they would all be together. Even if she only had seven years with them, those were seven amazing years full of love and care. She should've had many more.

Ryland was speechless for a minute, a look of pure sympathy filling his face as he slowed to a stop. He turned to her with a little shake of his head.

"I'm really sorry. I had no idea they passed during that dragon attack. I remember being in the orphanage that day and hiding under a table. It was a miracle that we survived," Ryland murmured softly, his shoulders dropping a little.

"They were just one of the unlucky ones. Gram heard what happened and took me from the orphanage to live with her outside of the Kingdom so that I would be around family," Violet told him, digging the toe of her boot into the ground, kicking a few leaves around mindlessly. It was strange telling someone about that incident, but it made her feel a little better to get it off of her chest. It was hard talking to Gram about it because she didn't want to make Gram upset. Violet lost her parents, and Gram lost her own daughter and son-in-law. They were both dealt hard blows that day, and the pain lingered.

"At least you were able to be with family. That's important," Ryland pointed out, a bit of a lost look appearing on his face. He glanced away before starting to walk again, his head turning to look longingly at the river as it veered the other way. He ducked under low hanging branches, vines and leaves brushing his hair as he moved.

Up ahead, the trees weren't as tall as some of the other ones in the forest. Some of their branches hung low and were covered with moss. There was no direct path, bushes and branches interfering with them heading straight forward. They had to be careful not to get turned around as they veered around obstacles.

"I feel like we're getting into a new environment," Violet murmured, glancing around at a plethora of new plants. The vines weren't green like usual. A lot of them were a light red color. The leaves on the bushes curved into a sharp point at the end, making Violet wary of anymore venomous plants around the area. She didn't spot the herbs that she normally would around her either.

Violet had a feeling that they were heading in the right direction, but it wasn't a straight shot to the cabin or the main path that she was used to. They would have to veer to the right or left to get exactly where they needed to go, which explained this odd territory. They just needed to get through it and then figure out which way to veer.

"This is unfamiliar to you?" Ryland asked her, a hint of worry in his tone as he turned to glance at her. If it was unfamiliar to her, it was incredibly unfamiliar to him. He had no idea what to expect from this place, but he knew that there would be danger. It would probably be just a little different than the danger in the other parts of the forest.

"It's just different. I'm sure it all plays by the same rules. We just have to be careful," Violet told him, trying to calm him down. If they panicked, they would have an even worse time trying to fight their way through here. She heard a slight shuffle of leaves up ahead, prompting her to reach out and grab Ryland's hand, halting him.

"Oh, great," Ryland huffed out quietly, already knowing what her motion meant. He froze in place, looking ahead toward a cluster of dark green bushes that were shaking a little due to something that they couldn't quite see yet.

"It seems big," Violet whispered, noting how the entire bush was shaking. Something small couldn't make it move like that. She leaned to the side a little, trying to peer through a space between the bushes to see what was moving. She caught a glimpse of something with dark fur and light brown stripes before jerking herself back into place before the creature saw her. It looked beast-like, and she didn't want to see the rest of it.

"We have to get up high into one of these trees," she whispered to Ryland, her hand still gripping the taut muscle of his upper arm. She turned her head to the left, seeing a tree about fifteen feet away that had a thick branch that sloped toward the ground. They could use it to climb up to the higher branches. She pointed to the tree and then looked back at Ryland, receiving a nod of understanding. This was another moment that she couldn't mess up, and she had never felt so petrified in her life.

Chapter Twelve

AMONG
THE TREES

"Run!" Violet hissed before taking off toward the tree, hearing Ryland right on her heels. She heard the bushes behind them rustle wildly, followed by a guttural growl that made her heart drop into her stomach. Part of her wanted to look back at the beast as it panted heavily and tried to chase them down. A bigger part of her willed her to run as fast as she could without looking back.

Once she reached the tree branch, Violet ran up along it, watching her steps as much as she could until she fell into an awkward crawl to get up the rest of the branch toward the thick trunk. She reached behind her to grab Ryland's hand, helping him climb up the sloped branch faster so that they could crouch near the trunk together.

"What is that thing?" Ryland gasped out as he gazed down at the beast, which was bigger than any wolf that Violet had ever caught a glimpse of. It ran on four legs, had a short tail, had massive paws with three toes and long claws, and its face looked almost smashed in. It was almost a mix of something canine and something feline. The canines in its large mouth were so long that they stuck out of its mouth, while its eyes were small and beady, and the ears looked sharp and pointed.

"I'm just going to call it a beast. I have no idea what it actually could be. I've never seen one before!" Violet exclaimed, shaking her head in disbelief as she sat there and caught her breath. Her eyes trailed the beast as it circled the trunk of the tree, growling steadily as it gazed up at them.

"I'm glad it can't climb," Ryland finally chuckled after a moment, placing his hands behind his head as he straddled the branch to keep from falling off. He breathed in deep as he turned to her, unable to help but share a relieved laugh with her. That had been another close call, and they could only hope that the beast would decide to leave soon.

"I was a bit worried about that, but it's too big to get up here," Violet replied, pointing out the beast's stocky and muscular build. It would have a hard time hauling itself up the sloped branch to where they were at, and she guessed that it wasn't a very good jumper.

"We need to get out of this area of the forest as soon as we can," Ryland told her, gazing around at the area surrounding them, like he expected some other threat to come thrashing through the bushes. It was a warranted concern.

Violet nodded, agreeing with his point. They could only protect themselves so much with one knife. It would probably feel like jabbing at the beast with a stick because it was so burly. She hoped that this stretch of forest didn't span for awhile because she wasn't sure how long they would fare here. She took a sip from the water canteen before handing it over to Ryland, a stressed sigh sounding from her as the beast laid down at the base of the tree trunk.

"Well, we can't really leave this tree until it decides to leave," Violet muttered, wishing the beast wasn't so adamant about sticking around. It was either too tired to leave right now or too hungry to let a good meal get away. They couldn't stay up in this tree for too long. They only had water and no food, which wouldn't last them long at all. She pushed her blonde hair behind her shoulders, wishing that she had something to tie it up with.

"I think this forest is trying to make sure that we don't leave," Ryland groaned, his eyes rolling up toward the blue sky beyond the tree leaves. Every path had some sort of hard obstacle that they had to face, and the obstacles weren't getting any easier. How many times did they almost have to die before they could leave this place?

"It's sparing my life for another day or two," Violet smirked, holding the branch between her thighs tightly so that she wouldn't slip off. She traced a few patterns in the branch's wood with her forefinger mindlessly, wondering whether the forest would kill her or the King. Both options were promising on that aspect.

"I don't want you to die," Ryland told her as he shifted his eyes back to hers. There were only a few inches of space between them as they faced each other on the branch. He sighed heavily, parting his lips to speak again.

"Ever since I grew up in the orphanage, I wanted to help people. That's all the kids did in there was help each other because we had no one except each other. The older boys protected me, showed me how to protect myself, and then I wanted to protect other people who couldn't defend themselves," Ryland started to explain, waving one hand around in animated motions as he spoke.

Violet nodded, not saying anything and merely listening. She wanted to know why he chose the path that he did. He could've been anything else, but he chose to be a bounty hunter. Granted, he sounded like he was a successful one, but it was still a treacherous position to hold. He had too much kindness to remain a bounty hunter, and she wondered if he knew that or not.

"I wanted to join the guards. I used to watch them march, and I watched them fend off that dragon. I wanted to be them, so when I was old enough, I tried to become one. Little did I know, they like their guards to have a certain background. A poor orphan wasn't what they were looking for," Ryland continued with a saddened look, one that struck Violet deep.

Violet knew that Ryland couldn't control his background and upbringing. Once a person was old enough to leave the orphanage, that person left with nothing of their own. They had to start from scratch, including finding a job and a place to live. They had to climb all the way back up the ladder, having to fight for every opportunity that they possibly could.

"They told me that I could start off as a bounty hunter to prove my worth, to see if I could follow orders and take down criminals. I did that for years, capturing more criminals in a day than they did in a week. I thought that they would let me be a guard by now, but they just laugh at me and tell me to keep trying. I'm starting to think that they won't ever let me be a guard," Ryland muttered, his tone coming out a bit bitter as he stared down at the branch.

Violet frowned, not liking seeing him like this. He seemed so drained and deflated, and she wished that he could see how corrupt the royal family and the guards were, especially since they were obviously just toying with him.

"I'm sorry they've been treating you that way, but they're never going to let you be a guard. They still see you as a poor orphan, and they always will because they're horrible people. They care about no one but themselves, and you're better than that," Violet told him firmly, needing him to believe that. There were better ways to help people than to serve the worst people in the Kingdom. The royal family caused the problems that Ryland wanted to protect people from. He was trying to adhere to the wrong side of the issue.

Ryland gave his head a little shake, a frown adorning his face.

"I don't think I'm better than anyone. That's the only thing I've thought of doing since I was growing up. I wouldn't know what to do with myself if I gave that up," Ryland explained to her, looking completely lost.

Violet nodded, understanding his dilemma. It was scary having to start all over, but that was sometimes the best thing to happen. She was terrified of leaving the cabin, which had been her home for so long, but she knew that being as far away from the Kingdom as possible was the safest thing to do. Some sacrifice was necessary in the name of safety.

"You could start over. That's what I'm doing. Don't think of it like the end. Think of it like the beginning," Violet told him, hoping to shift his perspective to one that was more positive. Starting over could be something really great for him. He could reevaluate what he wanted to do with his life because he was still young. He didn't have any attachments to the Kingdom. In fact, it would be best if he just left the Kingdom entirely.

"Aren't you scared of doing that? Leaving everything behind? You'll have nothing at first," Ryland asked her, looking unsure.

"I'm petrified, but I'll be less worried knowing that I'm far away from a Kingdom that wants nothing more than to kill me and the only family that I have left," Violet pointed out.

"I just don't know what I would do," Ryland told her honestly, shrugging his shoulders.

"It's okay to not know everything. Just focus on what you do know, which is that you want to help people," Violet offered the piece of advice to him, wanting him to find his way back to the source of his drive and motivation. That was the easiest way for him to figure out what his next step needed to be.

"Am I capable of that? Helping people? If all those criminals I turned in were people like you … people who were just trying to survive with no ill will … am I just a bad guy?" Ryland sighed, giving her a worried look. He looked incredibly concerned if that was actually the case. He didn't want to be the person that he tried to protect people from.

Violet reached out to him before she could think about the action, her hand resting on top of his. She gave his hand a comforting squeeze as she shook her head with a small smile.

"I don't believe that you're a bad person. You're just doing the wrong thing for the right reasons. You saved me, so you helped me," Violet pointed out, her smile brightening as one of his own started to cross his lips. She knew how confusing it could be to figure out his entire life, but he had to at least take one step in the right direction. Then, everything else would fall into place.

"Thank you … for listening and everything. I haven't really told people anything about that … or anything," Ryland admitted to her, gazing down at their joined hands. He drifted his thumb over her knuckles gently.

"It was the same way with me. What happened with your parents? You never mentioned them," Violet had to ask, feeling too curious to pass that topic over. She wondered if his parents passed away when he was young like her own. She didn't wish that pain on him at all.

Ryland chuckled dryly.

"Evidently, they ditched me at the orphanage soon after I was born. The people at the orphanage raised me until I had to leave," Ryland replied.

"Oh … that's awful," Violet murmured, unable to find anymore words to say to him. It actually made an ache echo through her chest after hearing that. She couldn't imagine her parents just tossing her away like that. It seemed cruel.

"The guards don't want me. My own parents don't want me. No one wants me," Ryland laughed out, but the tone bordered on painful. He tried to feign a smile, one that tried to say that he didn't care, but Violet could see right through it.

Violet placed her other hand over his, gripping him tight so that he would look at her.

"That's not true. Don't think that you're not worth something because you are. You're worth something to me," Violet blurted out the words, her cheeks burning steadily. She didn't want him to think of himself as worthless because she believed that he was a good person deep down. She believed that they connected in some sort of deep way, sparking up a level of concern and care that she had for him. She didn't want anything bad to happen to him, and that told her enough about her own feelings for him.

Ryland squeezed her hand, thanking her in the motion. He glanced down at the beast and then up, his eyes widening a little in thought.

"We should get some rest while we're stuck up here. Those two tree branches are close together. We can sit on them and lean back against the trunk," Ryland suggested as he nodded to two branches right above them.

Violet looked up, breaking away from the warm moment. She was sure that it would return eventually. She saw the limbs that he was talking about and nodded, able to reach up and grab one of them. She hauled herself onto one, moving over so that he could follow her and sit on the right most one. She leaned back against the trunk, her right leg hanging off of the side of the limb as Ryland sat on the one next to her.

"I'm afraid of falling asleep and then falling off," she laughed softly, giving him a sheepish smile.

"Lean against me. We'll nap in shifts so that we can keep each other from falling off," Ryland suggested, motioning to his shoulder.

Violet nodded, giving him a thankful smile before leaning her head against his shoulder. She let her eyes flutter shut, relaxing into him as he made sure that she didn't slip off and fall. Despite them starting on different sides, she felt a lot closer to him now. There were things that they shared, pain that they understood, and it showed her that even people who started as far apart as possible could still come together if they tried hard enough.

Chapter Thirteen

VILLAGE IN
THE HILLS

By the time the beast gave up and left the base of the tree, it was nearly nighttime, and they weren't going to risk traveling through this area of the forest during the night. Being around there during the daytime had proven to be dangerous enough. They took turns napping throughout the day, resting up and conserving as much of their energy as they could since they only had water to drink and no food to eat. Each hour felt like it dragged on, draining them steadily.

"I want to go to a village in the hills," Violet murmured tiredly, her arm pressing to his as they leaned against each other from the branches. She rolled her neck a little to loosen it before leaning her head back against the trunk. Since they had slept through so much of the day, they were fairly awake during the midst of night into the very early hours of the morning, darkness cloaking them everywhere. They could hardly even see each other through it, relying on touch to keep track of each other.

"A village in the hills? That sounds nice. Where'd that come from?" Ryland chuckled, his shoulders shaking out of amusement at her random comment. It had been so quiet for about ten minutes that he had thought that she had fallen asleep again.

Violet cracked a smile, tilting her head back to think about that imaginary village that she always drew up in her mind. It seemed so far away from her, and it seemed to be shifting farther away on top of that, like it didn't want to be caught. All she wanted was to grab hold of it and never let it go.

"I've just always wanted to live somewhere peaceful like that. It may seem boring, but I could explore the hills and surrounding areas. I could actually make friends in the community and not be outcasted. I could be myself around people," Violet murmured, wishing for that lifestyle so badly. When she was younger and didn't understand how bad the royal family was, she begged Gram to take her to the Kingdom to visit it so that she could explore the shops and see her old friends. However, Gram refused, having to explain to Violet that she could be taken way from Gram and that Gram could be hurt. It was a hard lesson to comprehend, but she eventually got it.

"It doesn't sound boring to me. It sounds really nice actually," Ryland replied, moving to smile at her until he realized that she couldn't even see him. He shifted a little on the branch, accidentally throwing himself off balance and making him nearly topple over the edge.

"Woah, careful!" Violet gasped out, feeling him slip away from her. She looped her arm in his, anchoring him to her side so that he wouldn't fall. She caught her breath and hit him in the shoulder with her other hand.

"Ow! What was that for?" Ryland gritted out as he rubbed his shoulder, soothing the ache from her hit.

"For scaring me! Stop that," Violet sighed out, drawing in a deep breath to calm her rapid heart rate. She needed him to be careful.

Ryland smiled to himself, hearing the concern in her tone.

"Alright, alright. Looks like sunrise is coming soon," he told her, nodding to the gradually lightening sky to their left. He couldn't wait to get out of the tree and stretch. It was numbingly painful sitting up here for so long at that point. His leg fell asleep multiple times throughout the night.

"Finally. I actually can't wait to get away from the safety of this tree and down there in all of the danger that awaits us," Violet mused with a little laugh, wanting to walk around finally. She also hoped to find a berry bush or two to help hold them over until they got around some real food. She had never been so hungry in her life. It was a pain that she never wanted to feel again.

They waited for another two hours, watching the sunrise together as they sat in the tree with their arms locked together. The sight was a bit obstructed because of the trees, but it was still beautiful. The greatest part about it was them finally being able to climb out of the tree and get back on flat ground after hours of being stuck up there.

"Hold on. Let me make sure the area is clear," Violet whispered to Ryland as she crouched on the sloped branch. She peered over various bushes, searching for any sign of the beast. This was its area, so she knew that it had to be around here somewhere, but she didn't see it around right now. She waved Ryland down as she moved down the sloped branch and all the way down to the ground.

"Finally," Violet breathed out as she stretched every limb of her body, sighing in relief as she took a moment to acclimate to being back on the ground again. She watched Ryland twist and stretch his back, prompting a smirk onto her face. It was the small things that kept them going.

"Alright, let's get back," Ryland murmured, keeping his voice low like Violet. Danger lurked everywhere. He shifted the knapsack higher up on his back before motioning for her to follow him toward the rising sun. He crept through the bushes, looking tense as he glanced every which way.

Violet followed close behind him, nearly flinching at any strange sound that happened around them. They had to be on the alert, but they also needed to get out of here as quickly as they possibly could.

"We need to speed up," she whispered to Ryland, placing her fingertips on the knapsack to usher him forward a little faster.

Ryland nodded and quickened his steps, slipping past more trees and bushes, stepping over vines and roots. He narrowed his eyes as he spotted something up ahead, nodding to it and pointing.

"That's a blackberry bush, right?" He asked her, shifting to the side a little so that she could see past him.

Violet felt her stomach growl in response to the sight of the familiar berries.

"Yes," she replied, following Ryland over to it and pausing. They could take a quick break to eat and gather some more energy. Violet picked a few berries off of the bush along with him, wincing as the bush shook a little. She placed one berry between her lips, reveling in the sweet taste. She was torn. She wanted to savor each berry, but she knew that she needed to hurry up.

"After we get out of this forest, I'm never eating berries again," Ryland sighed after popping a few more berries into his mouth. Despite the growing aversion, he still picked a few more off of the bush to eat. They needed as much energy as they could conjure up for the journey ahead, and there was no telling how long that would be. He slipped the knapsack off of his back and placed it on the ground, leaning over on each side to stretch his back again.

"I doubt that you'll even set foot in a forest again," Violet laughed quietly before chewing on a few more berries. Once she left the forest, she probably wouldn't go back to another one for a little awhile. She needed a break from all of this danger and leafy clutter. She wanted open spaces, like hills, and places to purchase food instead of hunt for it all of the time.

"You're not wrong," Ryland chuckled as he placed another berry between his lips, his eyes shifting past her. Suddenly, his eyes widened, and he swallowed wrong, making him cough and choke on the berry.

"What? What is it?" Violet hissed, placing her hand on his shoulder to try to steady him. He needed to be quiet, but she knew that he couldn't really help himself choking on a berry. She patted his back, watching his hand shoot up to point behind her. She spun around to see the beast from yesterday stalking its way toward them, its teeth bared and glinting.

"Oh … no …," Violet breathed out, starting to back away from the beast as it continued to creep forward.

"Run!" Ryland shouted before taking her hand and whisking her off in the direction that they were heading. If they were going to run, they needed to run in the right direction. He tugged her along, hopping over roots and crashing through bushes.

Violet panted as she trailed him, hearing the beast thrash through the greenery behind them. She couldn't tell if the beast was catching up to them or not, but she was too afraid to turn around and look. She nearly stumbled on a vine, but she regained her balance quickly, her heart jumping into her throat at the close call.

"We need to lose it!" Ryland shouted back to her, his energy already sapping. It was difficult to run on no energy, and he found himself slowing down a little bit. His chest heaved heavily, his breathing turning faint.

Violet looked around for some sort of aid or escape for them. It had to come fast because her legs were aching and burning, her chest tightening from the energy exertion. Her eyes landed on a pair of trees up ahead. They grew close together, making a small gap that she and Ryland could probably just fit through, but the beast wouldn't be able to. The trees were surrounded on both sides by other trees, so the beast wouldn't easily be able to find a way around.

"Up ahead! The gap between the trees!" Violet called to him.

Ryland located the trees up ahead that she was talking about, a worried expression filling his face.

"Those? I don't know if I'll fit through!" Ryland replied, maintaining his pace as the trees came closer and closer. His upper body was fairly built, and the gap between the trees was pretty thin. If he even did make it, it would be an incredibly tight fit. However, there wasn't any other option for him besides giving up and curling up on the ground so that the beast could make a meal out of him.

"Try!" Violet told him, unable to think of any other plan in time. They had to at least attempt to slip through to safety.

Ryland breathed in deep as he approached the gap, his feet lifting off of the ground as he jumped through sideways, the tree trunks scraping his cheek and his back painfully. However, he made it through, tumbling onto the ground soon after.

Violet followed him through the gap, her knee catching one of the tree trunks and making her topple down on top of Ryland. She whipped around, her face filling with pure fear as she watched the beast leap toward the gap. She flinched as it smacked into the tree trunks before falling onto the ground with a heavy thud, its body not moving afterwards.

"Did it just knock itself out?" Ryland asked from under her, his eyes wide in bewilderment.

Violet nodded wordlessly, feeling completely speechless as she tilted her head up to gaze at its unmoving body on the other side of the trees. The plan had actually worked. She turned back to Ryland as she crouched above his legs, a laugh breaking from her.

"We have survived once again," she breathed out, ignoring the searing pain in her knee from it getting scraped. Even the fabric of her pants was horribly torn. To her surprise, she felt Ryland's arms around her in a sudden embrace, a laugh echoing from him. She found herself winding her own arms around his neck, hugging him close as he rocked her gently.

"How do we keep doing that?" Ryland murmured against her shoulder, his scraped cheek resting against her.

Violet's fingers mindlessly drifted up into his short hair as she smiled, knowing the answer to that already. It was a simple answer, one that she had known for quite awhile now.

"Because we have each other."

Chapter Fourteen

THE DAYS
ARE FOREVER

"Are you sure you're okay?"

"Yes, stop fretting," Ryland smirked as he playfully batted away Violet's hand from touching his scratched-up cheek. He walked at her side as they started to venture into terrain that was a bit more familiar. It looked more like the forest that they were used to, which lifted their spirits a little bit more.

A soft laugh broke from Violet as she lifted her hands in surrender. She couldn't help but act like that toward him. With every close death encounter, she found herself growing closer to him, wanting to protect him even more fiercely. It was a strange and new feeling, but she really felt like she genuinely liked him. When she gazed at him periodically during their walk, she felt something nearly flutter in her chest, like there were butterflies trapped inside. It was a warm and comforting feeling, one that she didn't want to let go of anytime soon. She wondered if he felt the same way about her, but she was too nervous to ask or bring up the topic.

"I think we're getting close to where we need to be," Violet told him, recognizing some of the vined plants and herbs that she normally saw on her walks through the forest. She just had to find the main path, and then she would know exactly where she was at and where she needed to go from there.

"I've never heard anything more relieving," Ryland chuckled, breathing out a sigh of relief as his body seemed to relax a little. There was more energy in his step, but it was from more of a mental energy boost than a physical one. He felt exhausted and drained, but he didn't want to stop until they got where they needed to be since they were so close now. He couldn't give up now.

"It feels like we've been out here forever, but it's only been a few days," Violet pointed out, hardly believing that even as she said it. A few days out in the forest felt like an eternity of dodging death and danger with a person who turned from her enemy to someone that made her heart hammer heavily in her chest. It was strange how so many of her original feelings changed when she got to know him. Like she expected, there was much more to him beyond the surface, and she was glad that she got to know the real him.

"It's definitely been some of the most interesting days that I've ever had," Ryland told her, flashing her a smile. They walked so close together that their hands periodically touched, coaxing them to pass each other shy looks every once in awhile. There was tension between them, but it didn't feel like the bad kind that made them uncomfortable. There were obviously unspoken words between them waiting to be revealed.

Violet stepped through a few bushes and turned her head a little to the left, noting how the greenery in that direction seemed to be shaped unnaturally, like someone had regularly cleared a path through that way.

"Wait, I think that's the path to my grandmother's place," Violet told him, pointing to the thin clearing in the growth. She stepped toward it, glancing each way to realize that it looked a bit familiar. They were definitely in the right place.

"Really? This looks familiar?" Ryland asked her, peering at the path that she was talking about.

Violet nodded, trying to figure out which way led to her grandmother's house. Maybe if she could take him there first, they could figure out what to do with the whole situation of taking her to the Kingdom. She hoped that she had possibly turned him off of that path. Before she could figure out which way to go, the bushes around one way of the path ruffled, two guards stepping through.

"I never thought our searches would actually be successful," one of the guards laughed out in pure disbelief. The one who spoke had a beard, while the other had a clean-shaven face. Both guards were tall and built large with heavy armor. They both had short swords holstered in their belts, and their hands were already placed on their handles.

"Isn't that the bounty hunter?" The clean-shaven guard asked, tilting his head a little in curiosity as he stared at Ryland.

"Ah, yes. Bringing her in, boy?" The bearded guard asked Ryland, his voice coming out gruff as he gestured him forward.

Ryland shared a concerned look with Violet, his body tensing up as he glanced between the guards and her. He looked confused and lost, unsure of what to say or do in that moment.

"Are you deaf? Why is she not restrained?" The bearded guard snapped at Ryland, taking a threatening step forward.

"I'm not taking her to the Kingdom," Ryland replied firmly, standing his ground as he broadened his shoulders.

Violet gazed at him in surprise, not expecting to hear him say that, but she was glad to. It just confirmed to her that he was actually on her side, which sent a flush of warmth through her face. She turned back to the guards, who looked bewildered. She knew that things were about to escalate, but she knew that Ryland had her back, while she had his. It was just another obstacle for them to jump over together.

"Then, we'll take you both to the King," The bearded guard growled before drawing his sword and pointing it toward them, the clean-shaven guard pulling the same move.

Ryland drew his knife, giving Violet a worried look when he remembered that she was weaponless. He shifted to move in front of her, giving the guards a warning glare to tell them to back off. Of course, they didn't listen.

Violet didn't want to stand behind Ryland and rely on him to protect her. She wanted to help him, prompting her to glance behind her, trying to find something to help. Her eyes soon landed on a broken tree limb. It was only as thick as her wrist and as tall as up to her knee when it was standing, but it would do. She hurriedly grabbed it and then lunged forward past Ryland before anyone else could react since no one expected her to move. She swung the branch, catching the bearded guard in the face and sending him stumbling sideways.

"Take him! I'll take the other!" Violet called to Ryland, figuring it would be smarter for him to take the bearded guard, who was far more aggressive, since Ryland had an actual weapon and not a broken tree limb. It seemed to be coming in handy, though. She deflected a swipe from the clean-shaven guard's sword with her branch, prompting her to shove his sword back toward him, the blade piercing his cheek. She drove her foot against his stomach, sending him right to the ground. She kicked his sword away from him before swinging the branch down at him.

The guard threw his arms up to deflect the branch, but his block was only shoved back against his own face, the back of his head striking the ground hard.

Ryland pitched a quick look over his shoulder to check on Violet, realizing that she was doing just fine with a tree branch. He turned back toward the bearded guard just in time to sidestep a jab from his sword. Ryland jumped on the opportunity to jab his knife against the guard's arm, making him cry out in pain as Ryland jumped back.

Violet stumbled off of the clean shaven guard's limp body, shifting the tree branch in her hands as she turned to look toward Ryland's way as he easily danced around the bigger guard's attacks. She took the moment to catch her breath, unable to help but admire Ryland as he jabbed and cut at the guard until he was brought to his knees in front of Ryland, blood dripping from the wounds.

Ryland dealt a few heavy punches to the unprotected areas of the guard's face until he crumbled to the ground. He shook his hand, trying to quell the ache as he stepped away from the guard, his breaths coming out quickly and hard.

"Talk about having a hard head," he grunted as he tried to massage his hurt knuckles.

Violet made her way over to him, gently taking his hurt hand. His knuckles looked red and nearly swollen, promising bruises for tomorrow.

"Let me take you to the cabin. It's just this way," Violet told him, nodding down the path. She was pretty sure that it was that way since the guards came from the other way from the Kingdom. She figured they needed to rest, and Gram could heal his hurt hand. She heard a soft groan from one of the guards, coaxing her to motion for him to hurry up and follow her. She didn't want to be around when the guards actually woke up.

Ryland nodded, glancing at the guards before letting her lead him up the path to Gram's cabin. He wiped the blood off of his knife blade on the inside of his coat before tucking it in his holster on his belt, his hand jerking back in pain at the motion.

"I can't believe you stood up to them," Violet breathed out, flashing him a proud look over her shoulder. He had been so strong, standing up to the people who he used to want to stand with. He finally turned his back on injustice, siding with her instead.

"I just … couldn't let them take you. I can't do that," Ryland replied with a shake of his head, looking surprised at himself as well. A shocked laugh broke from him, his eyebrows lifting in wonder.

Violet smiled at him, feeling multiple emotions thunder through her. She couldn't even fathom the feelings, but she liked how warm they all felt. She weaved around a few bushes, leading him straight until she came upon the cabin's clearing, a sigh of relief drifting from her. She was finally back home for now.

"Here it is," Violet told him before running forward, needing to find Gram. She had worried over her so much over the past few days, hoping that she kept herself safe and had enough food. She opened the door to the cabin, leading Ryland inside as she called for Gram's name. At first, Violet was greeted by silence, but after a few more calls, a familiar voice emerged from the hallway door.

"Violet? Is that really you?" Gram called out as she poked her head out of the doorway, a confused look gracing her face. She seemed shaken up, looking tired with disheveled hair and dark crescents beneath her eyes, like she hadn't been sleeping.

"Gram," Violet breathed out before embracing Gram gently, being careful of the older woman's increasingly frail nature. It felt good to be back in her arms, where she had fled to when things got bad since she was a little girl.

"Where have you been? Who is this?" Gram asked once they parted, looking confused as she glanced at Ryland and then back at Violet, not fully understanding what was going on.

Violet frowned as she gazed at Gram, feeling bad that she had caused her such distress. She had wanted to get back sooner, but the forest had been trying to keep her away, and then the guards searching around so close for her worried her. She had never seen them come so close looking for her, and she suspected that would only get worse.

"I tried to steal from the Kingdom's gold room. Well, I actually did it. I wanted to get enough so that you and I could move far away from here to somewhere safe. The guards are close to finding this place," Violet explained before gesturing to Ryland to hand her the knapsack. Her eyes shifted from his to his shoulders, noticing finally that he didn't have the knapsack with him.

"I … I think I left it by the blackberry bush when the beast chased us," Ryland nearly whispered the words, a guilty look crossing his face as he shook his head. He almost looked nauseous, his eyes avoiding Violet's.

As disappointed as she was about losing the gold, Violet couldn't bring herself to be mad at him because she knew that he didn't do it on purpose. She would just have to figure out something else to get her and Gram to that paradise village. She swallowed hard and nodded before turning back to Gram, who looked astonished.

"Ryland was a bounty hunter assigned to capture me and bring me to the King. We pretty much fought the forest to get back here, and he switched sides for me. He even fought the guards that we ran into for me," Violet explained, not wanting Gram to see Ryland as an enemy, despite him starting off as one.

Gram took a few moments to take in everything before smiling and nodding with a deep sigh.

"I didn't get a malicious feeling from him. I sense that he's hurt, though," Gram murmured before patting Violet's cheek affectionately and moving toward Ryland.

Ryland looked a little nervous, a small smile crossing his lips as he greeted Gram quietly.

"Violet has told me a lot about you," he told her.

"It seems like she has plenty more to say about you," Gram laughed softly beneath her breath before gently taking Ryland's hand, her eyes shutting soon after.

Ryland tensed up as he looked down at his hand and then at Gram, a confused look gracing his face as he felt something strange and warm. When Gram released his hand, he lifted it to gaze at it and flex it, noting how the redness and soreness was gone.

"Woah … thank you," Ryland breathed out, blinking in shock.

"You're stronger than you believe that you are," Gram told him, flashing him a wink and leaving him stunned on the spot.

Violet couldn't help but crack a smile, glad that Ryland had his first magical experience. She turned back to Gram, giving her a thankful look for welcoming Ryland. She knew that Ryland didn't experience that feeling much.

"Let me make some tea and you can tell me everything about what happened," Gram told them, giving them a warm smile before shuffling into the kitchen with her staff to make some herbal tea for all of them.

Violet nodded and led Ryland over to the rug in front of the fireplace, motioning for him to sit down next to her. She placed her hands up near the fire, reveling in its warmth and the comfort in general of being in an actual building again. She didn't ever want to take it for granted ever again after all that she had been through.

"What an adventure," Violet sighed out, coaxing a shared laugh between them. It felt like things were finally falling into place with them being back at the cabin, but the adventure had just started, along with the danger.

Chapter Fifteen

BREAK IN AND
BREAK DOWN

After having a long talk into the night and a decent dinner, Violet fell asleep in her bed at last, while Ryland was set up on the rug in front of the fireplace with plenty of blankets and a soft pillow. It was strange not having him sleeping next to her, but she was glad that they would wake up the next morning and not have to worry about something eating them.

When she finally did stir later in the morning, Violet blinked her eyes open slowly, a wide smile crossing her face automatically as memories flooded back to her mind. She and Ryland were finally safe at last, and he had chosen her over the King. What did that mean for them now? She pressed her teeth into her bottom lip anxiously, knowing that it was a topic that she wanted to talk to him about. She thought of him as more than a friend in her heart and mind, and she wondered if he felt the same way.

With the gold being lost, Violet faced another dilemma. How could she get her and Gram away from the cabin? Perhaps, Ryland would want to come along and could help. Maybe they could come into more gold. She nearly groaned at the clash of thoughts in her head, a soft sigh breaking from her. She would figure out her next step eventually. For now, she just wanted to talk to Ryland, hoping he had slept well last night.

Violet slipped out of bed and changed out of her sleep clothes, pulling on black pants and a white shirt with the sleeves cut off. She brushed through her hair, pulling the strands up into a ponytail with a red hair tie. After taking in a steadying breath, her cheeks already starting to warm up, she left her room quietly and crept down the hallway. Gram's room was down at the other end of the hallway, and her door was still closed, so she was still asleep. She headed into the living room to see Ryland still laying on the floor in front of the fireplace, nestled under thick blankets.

Ryland must've been awake because he lifted his head when Violet came close, a tired smile crossing his lips.

"Good morning," he murmured as he moved to sit up, stretching his arms above his head. His hair was a bit matted in the back and sticking up in various places, but he still looked good to Violet, who matched his smile.

"Hey, did you sleep well?" Violet asked him as she sat down next to him on the rug in front of the fireplace. The fire had died out long ago, but Gram would reignite it whenever she woke up. For now, the space was dimly lit by the sunlight streaming in through the windows.

"I did. It was nice to be back inside again. I think just knowing that I didn't have to constantly watch my back helped me fall right asleep," Ryland chuckled quietly as he drew a hand through his hair, ruffling up the back and smoothing down the front. He looked over at Violet with a warm look, a few moments of comfortable silence being shared between them.

Violet felt something inside of her stir, her thoughts shifting to what she had pondered on talking to him about earlier when she woke up. This would be a good moment. They had the time to themselves, and she felt brave enough to talk about it now.

"I wanted to talk to you about something … about how I've been feeling lately," Violet started, her eyes drifting down to the wooden floor out of shyness. It was hard not to feel nervous. She had never talked or acted on such feelings before because she had never felt them before. She hoped that he felt the same way, but she wasn't entirely sure. He could just be really nice.

Ryland straightened up a little as he nodded, an intrigued look crossing his face as he gazed at her.

"Alright, what is it?" He asked, a hint of excitement in his tone as he waited for her to talk to him.

Violet lifted her eyes to see him gazing at her expectedly, driving her nerves through the ceiling, but it was too late to back out now. She had to spill what was on her mind because it nearly felt like torture to keep those thoughts bottled up for so long. She parted her lips to speak, to reveal how much she had grown to like him, until she heard a sharp thud against the front door. She whipped around, pushing herself to her feet as she stared at the front door.

Ryland jumped to his feet, tossing the blankets off as he tensed up as another loud sound came from the door.

"I'm guessing that's not your grandmother," he whispered, watching the door shake a little from the impact of the hits, like someone was heavily kicking the door.

Violet couldn't even speak, confusion and fear striking her. She could only shake her head, her body freezing up as she listened to light commotion from outside of the cabin. She had no idea what was happening, but she knew that it wasn't a good thing and that she needed to move.

Suddenly, the door frame cracked, wood splintering as the door flew open, revealing a group of four guards. The one who had kicked the door down stepped through the doorway, a smirk crossing his face.

"There you are," he murmured, gazing at the two of them.

Violet's first instinct was to run, but she couldn't leave Gram all alone and vulnerable. She had to stay and fight, prompting her to run to the kitchen. She gripped the handle of one of the kitchen knives in the knife holder, yanking the thick blade out of its slot. She whipped around only to get struck by a heavy blow to her cheekbone by the first guard's hand, making her stumble off balance into the kitchen counter. She shook her head, trying to clear the glistening stars shining in front of her eyes.

"You thought that you could run and hide from us forever, didn't you?" The guard cackled at her, a wicked smile curving up across his stubbled face.

Violet rested her back against the kitchen counter, noticing another guard start to head toward her as the rest went for Ryland. She couldn't believe how trapped she was, and the path out of this situation wasn't clear to her. All she knew was that she had to fight harder than she ever had before. She struck at the guard with her foot, knocking him back against the counter before swiping at the thin guard lunging at her with her knife.

The thin guard ducked under her strike, his fist driving up against her stomach to knock the breath from her. He grabbed her arms and tossed her down onto the kitchen floor.

Ryland glanced Violet's way worriedly, hearing a lot of commotion from the kitchen as the two guards went after her. He was struggling himself, jabbing at the guards facing him as much as he could to try to ward them off.

Violet scrambled to her feet as the thin guard drew his short sword, narrowly missing a stab. She countered with her knife, digging the blade into the guard's waist in a gap in his armor.

As the thin guard howled in pain, the other guard reached for Violet from the ground, trying to push her away from the thin guard.

With an angered shout, Violet kicked him back against a wooden cabinet, the wood splintering upon impact. A rush of victory surged through her as she watched the stubbled guard slump down against the ground, but the warm feeling didn't last. She felt a sharp pain in her stomach, like someone punched her, but the pain lingered. She looked down to see the tip of the thin guard's sword piercing her body, her breathing halting for a few seconds out of shock.

"No!" Ryland cried out as he stood over one body, the other guard struggling to get to his knees behind him. He met Violet's eyes briefly before she crumbled to the ground, the blade slipping from her body as she hit the ground on her back with a pained huff. He slammed his fist against the remaining guard's face, sending him to the ground. Ryland moved to stand up and rush over to Violet, but he paused as Gram limped into the kitchen.

"You're not welcome here," Gram gritted out at the thin guard, her balance and strength wavering a little as she leaned on her staff.

"It's about time you rogues were brought to justice," the thin guard gritted out, stepping over Violet as she lay crumbled on the ground to head toward Gram in a threatening manner.

An amused smile slowly crossed Gram's face as she lifted her hand, her eyes steadily closing.

Violet felt a light tremor of energy pass over her, but it hit the thin guard full force, sending him flying back against the kitchen wall. A shocked look crossed her face as she looked back at Gram, her vision starting to darken and blur with every passing minute. The pain was excruciating, aching throughout her entire body, but she did everything that she could do to stay awake as blood steadily welled up through her fingers as she put pressure on her wound.

Gram collapsed to her knees after she casted the spell, a pained sound breaking from her as her strength and energy sapped. She crawled closer to Violet, a worried look adorning her face.

"Oh, dear," Gram sighed softly, her hand reaching over to gently place itself on Violet's cheek.

Violet gritted her teeth, feeling herself start to slip toward darkness. It was so hard to hold on, but she focused on the feeling of Gram's hand on her cheek, tears soon slipping from her eyes.

"It hurts …," she breathed out weakly, wishing that the pain would just go away. The agony was overwhelming enough to drown in, and she was losing the strength to swim.

Ryland rushed to Violet's other side, his hand coming over to grab her free one.

"Hey … hey … it's okay," he whispered, trying to put on a comforting smile, but he looked utterly terrified as he gazed at her.

Gram patted Violet's cheek softly before removing Violet's hand from her wound and replacing it with her own.

"I love you, Violet. I'm so grateful for our time together, how you let an old woman teach you a thing or two, how you took care of us. Now, I want to take care of you. I have to protect *you*," Gram murmured to Violet, tears filling the bottom of her eyes before she closed them.

Violet started feeling something warm and strong flowing through her body, focusing mainly on her wound. It felt different than Gram just healing her, though.

"What are you doing?" Violet asked, her voice coming out shaky as she watched Gram start to wilt over. More tears broke from her eyes as her pain started to disappear, but a new kind of agony took place as Gram paled.

"Gram, no! Stop!" Violet cried out, realizing that Gram was giving Violet the rest of her life, the rest of her energy, to save her. She didn't want Gram to sacrifice herself for her, making her reach out and grab Gram's shoulder, but Gram soon toppled to the ground, remaining still.

"No … no!" Violet sobbed, lifting her hand to her mouth as she cried, her body shuddering with sadness. She had felt like this when her parents passed away. Now, she had no family, leaving her alone.

"I'm so sorry … I'm so sorry," Ryland murmured into Violet's hair as he embraced her, rocking her gently as she continued to cry.

"She's gone … I can't believe she's gone," Violet whimpered into Ryland's chest, wanting to bury herself there forever. She felt safer in his arms, able to momentarily escape from the terrible world around her and the losses that she continued to endure.

Chapter Sixteen

NO MORE ATTACHMENTS

After pulling herself together long enough to lock up the guards in the basement and lay Gram in her bedroom until they could figure out where to bury her, Violet sat down in front of the fireplace and refused to move for hours. There wasn't a fire in the fireplace for a while until Ryland lit one and then sat down next to her after ensuring the guards couldn't escape the basement. He didn't say anything to her for a while, letting silence settle between them as they watched the fire dance and sway in front of their eyes.

"Everything fell apart so fast. I don't know what to do now," Violet finally whispered, knowing that she needed to speak the clashing thoughts in her mind. It was dangerous for her to trap them up in there for so long, despite them being nearly unbearable to talk about. It felt like her entire life had crumbled before her eyes, and the path that she originally envisioned was gone. She was truly lost mentally and emotionally, and she didn't know how to come back from that.

"She would want you to be safe," Ryland told her, a sympathetic look filling his face. He moved to sit closer to her, his shoulder brushing hers. Slowly, he reached out to gently take her hand, wanting to support her in any way that he could.

"I'm not safe here," Violet sighed out, knowing that was still the case. She still couldn't stay here. She just wouldn't have Gram with her on her journey away from the Kingdom, and that killed her inside. She didn't want to do this all alone, facing the road ahead without a guide and familiar comfort. It made her want to curl up and give up, letting the King do what he wanted to her. It was hard to care when she was losing everything that she loved.

"But I can't leave … I can't possibly make it out of here on my own," Violet muttered with a shake of her head. She glanced over at Gram's rocking chair that she always sat in before jerking her head back forward, unable to look at anything that reminded her of Gram. Unfortunately, in the cabin, that was basically everything. It was hard to escape the memories that ghosted through the space.

"It's more dangerous to stay. If the King gets you … you're as good as dead. He's felt like he's lost too much to you to let you walk," Ryland explained, the corners of his mouth turning down in a deep frown.

Violet guessed that much. The King was not a merciful person. He ruled with a hard fist, one that struck anyone who dared to cross him in any capacity. If she were captured, she would never make it out alive, but trying to venture all of the way to a new village could get her killed too. It seemed like a long and happy life with her dying of old age wasn't in her favor right now.

"At least I gave him hell. I have nothing else to lose now if he captures me," Violet pointed out, shrugging her shoulders a little. It wouldn't be fun to die, but at least she would be back with her family and away from the Kingdom. Death honestly didn't sound like a bad concept at the time.

Ryland moved his hand to firmly grip her shoulder, drawing her hazy eyes to his hard ones.

"Hey, don't talk like that. You're not giving up. You're doing this for Gram," Ryland told her sternly, even narrowing his eyes a degree at her.

"I'm supposed to be doing what?" Violet asked him, wondering what he was talking about. It seemed like all of her future plans were completely gone at this point. There was no point in trying to pursue them anymore, and everything would hurt less if she just stopped trying to pursue them.

"Leaving this place behind and finding that village that we talked about," Ryland reminded her with a hint of a hopeful smile. She had spoken so highly of that place, a dream to turn to reality, and it sounded like she was letting go of it.

"I can't possibly do that alone! I'll get killed on the way or end up homeless and starving when I get there because I'll have no money," Violet fretted, burying her face in her hands. Despite Gram being old, she was a witch. She could draw up protective spells and help them make it through the long journey to wherever they decided to go. Violet could fight, but she only had so much energy and strength to spare.

Ryland embraced her tightly, holding her to his chest as she shook her head. He placed his hand on the back of her head, drawing his fingers through her soft hair.

"You're stronger than you think you are," he repeated Gram's words to her, meaning every single one of them. He gripped her arms gently before pulling her away from his chest so that he could meet her eyes. His hands drifted up to cup her face, his thumbs ghosting over her skin in comforting motions.

"Don't let them win. They don't deserve to win over you," he told her firmly, setting his jaw tight.

Violet knew that he was right, that she didn't need to roll over and submit to people she despised so easily. The last thing that she wanted to do was to give them the satisfaction of winning over her, putting her six feet deep in the ground for trying to survive. That kind of ending wasn't meant for her story, and she refused to make it a reality for her, but she felt so alone and scared. If she could find the path ahead, it was dark and dangerous, one that she wasn't sure that she could handle by herself. Despite everything in her life, she had never been all alone.

"I don't even know where to go," Violet muttered, her eyes dropping from his as she leaned into his touch. She didn't mind having his hands on her, especially as they comforted her. She didn't want to lose that feeling.

"Take the main road away from the kingdom and see where it leads you," Ryland told her, a bittersweet look adorning his face. His gaze drifted down to her lips and then back up to her eyes, a soft sigh breaking from him.

"I'll miss you," Ryland admitted, a hint of sadness tainting his small smile, like he wanted to be happy for her deep down.

Violet gave him a sad look, one mixed with confusion. She wondered what he was going to do, what his next move would be. She couldn't imagine him trying to be a guard or remaining a bounty hunter anymore, so she had no idea what was in store for him. Truthfully, she didn't want to part from him, wishing that they could remain together. Their paths had crossed, and she didn't want them to be separated any time soon if it all.

"What about you? What are you going to do?" Violet asked him, lifting one hand up to press over his.

Ryland shrugged a little with a sheepish smile.

"I really don't know. I don't really have any attachment to the Kingdom anymore. I don't need to seek approval from them," Ryland muttered with a shake of his head.

Violet pondered on his words, an idea coming to her mind, but she was afraid to suggest it. She didn't want to be too forward and lose the relationship that they were developing. That would kill her inside to lose the one friend that she had, the only person left in her life. However, she could lose him by not taking a chance and asking.

"Why don't you leave the Kingdom? Why don't you … come with me?" Violet asked him, hope filling her eyes as they rested on his. She knew that was asking a lot, especially since they only met a few days ago, but they had bonded closer than people who knew each other for years. They were connected, drawn together by danger and adventure. It seemed only right to continue that with each other.

Ryland gave her a shocked look, his lips parting, but no words came out for a few seconds.

"I … really? You would want me to come with you?" Ryland asked her, complete disbelief in his words.

Violet smiled at him and nodded, able to easily imagine them making it to the village together. They could continue to fight together to reach a place of peace, which they both strived for. They wanted a place where they could be themselves and find themselves. The Kingdom was not the place for them to do that.

"Of course. I don't want to be apart from you. We're … a team," she pointed out, feeling like they were a unit. It would feel unnatural to be apart, to take two different paths away from each other.

"You're right. We are a team. I'd love to come with you," Ryland murmured, drifting his thumb over her cheek affectionately. He gently rested his forehead against hers, his eyes fluttering shut as they took the moment to just be close to one another. Through all of the craziness, it was hard to find a second of peace to share with one another.

Violet let her eyes slide shut, reveling in his touch and the fact that she would no longer be alone. It was the most relief that she had felt in awhile, lifting some of the weight off of her shoulders. She drew in a deep breath, separating herself from reality for a few seconds before letting it all rain back down on her. As much as she wanted to sit here with him, she knew that they had work to do if they wanted to flee.

"We should bury Gram and then figure out a plan," Violet told him, opening her eyes back up. She had avoided burying Gram, afraid of feeling that pain hit her all at once. However, Gram deserved a burial and to be put at rest. Violet owed that to her for saving her life by giving her own.

"I'll find a spot to dig. You should say goodbye," Ryland replied gently. He pressed a soft kiss to her forehead before heading out of the cabin to find a shovel and dig Gram's grave.

Violet sighed softly and moved to head toward Gram's bedroom, her stomach gradually sinking with each step that she took in that direction. Part of her wanted to run away, but she had to be stronger than that. She needed to be her strongest right now, despite that being a lot to ask.

She opened Gram's bedroom door and stepped inside of the room, casting her eyes down toward the ground as she approached the bed slowly. She didn't want to look at Gram as she lay still and cold in the bed, but she needed to.

"I'm so sorry, Gram. I never meant for any of this to happen," Violet whispered before slowly lifting her eyes to Gram, a shaky breath leaving her. It was strange how at peace Gram looked, and Violet could only hope that she was in a peaceful place.

"Thank you for everything that you've done for me. You raised me, taught me, loved me. I could never repay you for everything that you've done for me, but I just want you to know that I love you," Violet breathed out, her bottom lip trembling as her eyes burned. She was surprised that she had any tears left over from earlier, but a few still slipped down her cheek. She reached out and placed her hand over Gram's gradually cooling one.

Violet closed her eyes, dropping her head down as she hoped for the best for Gram. She wasn't sure about reincarnation or the afterlife, but Violet hoped that Gram was happy wherever she did end up. Taking Violet in had been selfless. Raising Violet had been ambitious. Sacrificing herself for Violet had been brave. Gram was a lot of things, and Violet was grateful to have been raised by such a strong, talented woman. It helped craft her into the person that she was today.

A soft knock sounded from behind Violet, prompting her to wipe away her tears and turn to face Ryland. Her heart immediately dropped into her stomach because she knew what he was here to tell her. She didn't want to let go of Gram, to separate them by six feet. It felt too finalizing, like it really was the end of everything. However, Violet knew that she would soon face a new beginning, one that Gram would want her to have. She had to move forward for her, to live a life worth living out of the way of constant danger.

Ryland gave Violet a sympathetic smile, a sigh drifting from him as he nodded.

"It's time."

Chapter Seventeen

AMONG FLOWERS
AND HERBS

The funeral was harder than Violet expected it to be, constant tears coursing down her face as she gazed down into Gram's grave at her body. She adorned Gram with her favorite flowers, refusing to leave the grave looking so bare. It deserved to be dressed and decorated like Gram would want it. Gram loved nature, and Violet was determined to bury her surrounded by it.

Ryland stepped forward and helped Violet in any way that she wanted him to, adopting silence to let Violet grieve in quiet. He stood at her side and placed a hand on her shoulder out of comfort as Violet gazed down into the dressed grave.

"It looks beautiful. She would love it," Ryland murmured quietly.

A faint smile crossed Violet's lips as she nodded, believing that Gram would. Her body was adorned in a plethora of colorful flowers and herbs. She would've placed some of her favorite stones and gems in the grave with her, but those were down in the basement with the guards.

"I think so too. I hate to leave her here … but I know that she was always happiest here, despite the danger," Violet explained, knowing that Gram didn't want to leave her cabin deep down. When he was alive, Gram's husband had built the cabin for them. It would've been hard to separate Gram from such a memorable place. At least she could stay here in peace.

Ryland nodded as he listened, rubbing her arm gently.

"Whenever you're ready, I'll fill it in," he told her, not wanting to rush her.

Violet took one more long look at Gram, remembering every detail that she could before stepping back and nodding.

"Okay, I'm ready," Violet breathed out, blinking her eyes rapidly as she watched Ryland take the shovel and start filling in the grave. She felt her chest ache heavily, nearly paining her so much that it brought tears to her eyes. If it wasn't for Ryland, she would've completely fallen apart. At times, she felt like she still might, but she had to keep herself together for the journey ahead.

Once he patted down the dirt, Ryland stepped back, dropping the shovel onto the ground before turning to her.

"We should probably hurry and figure out a plan. The King will soon notice that the guards didn't come back," Ryland told her, pitching a wary look over his shoulder, like he expected more guards to come crashing through the brush.

Violet nodded, knowing they needed to run as fast as they could. It pained her that so much was lost from the last fight. Despite them beating the guards, Violet still felt like they ultimately lost, and that didn't sit well with her. She wanted to run from the Kingdom only after she obtained the upper hand, taking from the royal family what they deemed the most valuable, which was their gold. She had stolen it once. Who said she couldn't steal it again? She would desperately need some because they wouldn't be able to get by long without it.

"We need a plan … but not just to escape. We need a plan to take back what we lost … to show them that they haven't won," Violet murmured aloud, knowing that it probably sounded like nonsense to Ryland at first, but that was where her mind was at.

"What are you saying?" Ryland asked her, cocking his head a little out of confusion.

"Come on," Violet encouraged him, waving her hand to motion for him to follow her back inside of the cabin. She winded her way to her room and knelt by her bed to grab her map from under it. She placed it on her desk and then turned to him.

"I want to hurt them and help us. We need gold, and I want them to lose it," Violet told him, wanting to take away what they cared about the most since they did that to her. It was only fair. She tapped the castle on her map before parting her lips to speak again, knowing that he had plenty of questions.

"I know where the gold room is at. There are always two guards stationed outside. However, if we create a big enough distraction, we can draw all of the guards away, and I can grab as much gold as I can," Violet explained, building the plan in her head as she went. Since there were two of them, it would be easier to pull a plan like that off. She used to always have to only rely on herself, having to fight alone, but now she wasn't by herself. She had a partner that she trusted.

"How are we going to get the gold out of there?" Ryland asked her as he stepped up next to her side, giving her a little smile.

Violet could've hugged him, realizing how onboard he already was with her. He didn't doubt them. He had her back no matter what, and she couldn't believe how much she had been missing out on before she had met him. She felt true companionship and a sort of passion that she had never felt before with him.

"That's what I'm trying to figure out. We need something to transport it because I want to steal a large amount," Violet replied with a sigh, knowing that would be an issue that they would have to figure out. She had only been able to carry one knapsack full of gold, but she wanted to steal more than that. She wanted to hurt the royal family badly for all that they had put her through. No one ever kept the royal family in check, allowing them to rule in corrupt ways without any sort of consequences.

Ryland thought for a few moments before his expression brightened.

"I'll have that covered. What kind of distraction are we talking?" Ryland asked her, a devious look coming onto his face as he rubbed his hands together.

"Something big ... something disruptive," Violet laughed softly, tapping her forefinger against her chin. She had a few ideas to bounce with him, ones that were risky, but they would produce the best results for them. The distraction had to be big enough to draw most of the guards from the castle so that she could haul as much gold out of the gold room as she could.

The plan came together over the duration of a few hours, multiple lines and markers being written on the map to indicate routes and points of interest. It was in every way risky, but the reward could be so great for them. They would have enough gold to get them settled well in a new village, and it would deal a blow to the royal family. Money was the only thing keeping them powerful in the Kingdom besides their name. It would start their downfall.

Before they decided to go to bed, Violet found an old knapsack to start packing some of her things in. She couldn't bring a lot because, if everything went according to plan, she would leave the Kingdom after the heist and never look back. She could only have what she could carry on her back, so she packed a few clothes, three oranges that were leftover in the kitchen, and the love letter in her wardrobe.

When she pulled out the love letter, she paused, feeling a strong pull in her chest. Giving in, she looked down at it to read the handwritten words, already feeling a distinct ache echo through her chest.

My dearest Lillian,

You're sleeping as I write this. Today, we took the horses out to Stone Lake and spent the day there trying to catch minnows and collecting flowers. I never see you happier than when we're out exploring, so I'm planning another little adventure for us in the coming days. I'd do anything to keep a smile on your face. I've never felt such compassion for another human being before in my life. The amount of luck that I feel to just know you is immeasurable. Life was grey and cold before you became the fire of my life. I hope you know how loved you are. I hope there are infinite adventures awaiting us.

Until the next one,

Peter

Violet drew her eyes away from the letter, her hand lifting to rest over her chest as her heart thumped heavily within it. The words struck her more this time because she felt like she actually understood them. She had someone that she loved to go on adventures with, despite them being dangerous, and she enjoyed seeing him happy. She didn't like seeing him upset. She believed that she was falling for him, which scared her and excited her at the same time because it was new and strange.

"I packed my bag. Hey, you okay?" Ryland asked as he walked into her room, giving her a concerned look.

Violet folded the love letter and placed it in her bag before smiling at him and nodding.

"I'm great. I'm just ready to get started on our new adventure," she laughed softly, looking forward to the part where they got to the village and were able to settle down for a minute. It felt like one moment crashed into the next lately, and it was hard to find time to even catch a break.

"Me too. It's like we're starting new lives together," Ryland murmured, a soft, red glow adorning his face as he gazed at her. He seemed to shift shyly on the spot, while she moved in the same manner.

"Well, there's no one else that I would want to do that with," Violet replied, saying the words in a casual manner, but she felt the opposite. It wasn't a casual topic to her. It meant a lot, but she didn't want to scare him away or make things weird between them. She would rather have him as a friend than not at all.

"I feel the same way. If we can survive the forest, we can do this. I believe in us," Ryland told her, his hand reaching out to rest on her upper arm in an affectionate motion.

Violet felt her skin come alive just at his touch, her face already starting to warm. She was glad that they seemed to be on the same page, but she was still so afraid to just come out and tell him her feelings. They were emotions that she had never experienced before, and she almost didn't even know how to describe them.

"I guess we should get to bed soon. Big day tomorrow," Ryland commented, filling the silence that had settled between them. He also looked tired, a yawn soon breaking from him.

Violet nodded, needing to get as much rest as she could for tomorrow. There really wasn't much else that she could pack. She wished that she could take so much more, especially some things of Gram's, but that belonged to her. It was still her cabin.

"Goodnight," Violet murmured, watching Ryland lean close to press a soft kiss to her forehead, her eyes automatically fluttering shut at the touch. She loved the feeling and how safe it made her feel. It was paradise in a touch.

"Goodnight, Vi," Ryland whispered against her skin before smiling at her and heading out of her bedroom.

Violet drew in a deep breath, trying to quell the rapid and heavy beating of her heart. She moved her bag near her bed, smiling brightly to herself as her skin tingled. She wished that she had the courage to kiss him like that, to show him how she felt. She knew that she should soon because there was no guarantee that they would make it out alive tomorrow. Their lives hung in the balance, a delicate one, but she would do everything in her power to make the plan work. Their very future depended on it.

Violet changed into her sleep clothes before blowing out the candles lighting up her room and crawling into her bed. She stared up into the darkness, hoping that her dark end didn't await her tomorrow. There were so many things that she wanted to experience before it was her time to move on, and she wanted to do them with Ryland at her side. She wished for their safety, but she knew that blood would be spilled one way or another. Paradise required a blood sacrifice.

Chapter Eighteen

TOGETHER OR
NOT AT ALL

Violet gazed up at the cabin one more time, a faint sigh breaking from her lips. She adjusted her old knapsack on her back, the black material of her long sleeve shirt ruffling from the motion as it was tucked into dark pants and black boots under a black coat. She had to be a shadow today if she wanted to keep from getting caught red-handed.

"It's been nice," Violet voiced aloud, feeling a personal connection with the cabin. It was her home for so many years, which made it hard to leave behind. However, her new home would be safer, and that had to take precedence before her love for the cabin. She glanced around her, waiting for Ryland to return. He had left earlier that morning to take care of their transportation, telling her to trust him, which she did.

After another ten minutes, Violet heard leaves crackling from behind her. She placed a hand on the knife in her belt, whipping around to see Ryland moving through the brush toward her.

"Everything okay?" She asked him, wondering if he got everything prepared.

Ryland smiled at her and nodded, stopping and motioning for her to join him.

"Everything is ready. It's just down to us," Ryland told her, extending his hand out to her to take.

Violet breathed out a relieved breath as she placed her hand in his, letting him lead her through the forest away from the cabin and toward the Kingdom. It was still early morning, far before most were awake, and it would give them an edge.

"Are you ready?" Violet asked him as they walked side by side, their hands remaining joined. Part of her gushed over the sweet touch, while the other part worried about what was about to happen next. This might be the last time either of them would see each other alive, and that petrified her, making her body tense up.

Ryland seemed to feel her shift in demeanor, prompting him to squeeze her hand gently.

"I'm ready for our new lives no matter the risk," Ryland replied with a firm tone.

Violet nodded, glad that he was in the right mindset. It helped to look past the fear, to focus on the goal. She needed to shift her thoughts, to envision the end goal instead of the risks. That would just distract her.

"Please be careful," Violet told him, needing him to take as many precautions as he could. She couldn't lose him, and that wasn't even about the plan. She couldn't lose him in general or she would fall into pieces. With Gram passing, he had been the only thing keeping her together, reminding her that she was strong enough to do this. She couldn't lose sight of that.

"You won't lose me, and I won't lose you. Okay?" Ryland replied, meeting her eyes.

"Okay," Violet whispered, latching on to that belief with every fiber of her being. She bumped her shoulder against his, letting him lead her out of the forest and to a side entrance to the Kingdom that he knew of. It was over a stone wall, but footholds had been broken into the surface over the years. She wished that she had found it sooner, but Ryland normally used it as a faster way to get in and out of the Kingdom.

Ryland helped hoist her over the top before following her up and over, dropping onto the ground next to her behind a row of houses.

"I'm going to go ahead in front of you to kick off the distraction," Ryland told her, halting her behind a house.

"Alright, I'll wait for it before heading to the gold room," Violet nodded, drawing in a deep breath to steady herself. This whole plan was becoming more real by the second, and there would be no turning back soon. She couldn't and wouldn't abandon him when things started to get into motion.

Ryland reached up and rested a hand on the back of her neck under her hair, drawing her close to his body, his forehead dropping to hers.

"It's going to be okay. We'll be back together before you know it," he murmured the words softly, lifting his other hand to stroke her cheek in a comforting manner.

Violet wanted to stay in this position forever, reveling in the warmth and comfort of his hands. She met his eyes, feeling her heart hammer against her chest rapidly.

"I can't lose you. I'd lose a piece of myself," she whispered, unable to make her words come out any stronger than that. She rested her hands on his sides, holding him close to her and refusing to let go right now.

"You won't. I'll be right there with you," Ryland told her, his eyes dropping down to her lips. He met her eyes again briefly before crashing his lips against hers, his eyes closing as he leaned into the softness of her lips.

Violet's eyes widened in shock at first before gradually fluttering shut, her hands grabbing at him tighter. She reveled in how warm his lips were as they slowly pressed and moved against hers in soft touches. It almost felt like her heart was about to bust right out of her chest, but she loved the feeling of this. It was like getting even closer to him than she already had been. Eventually, she had to pull away to breathe, feeling like she was drowning in the kiss, a soft laugh breaking from her.

"We should've done that sooner," she murmured, her tone bittersweet. She loved how that was their first kiss, but she was petrified that it would also be their last. She wanted more of those moments, but they weren't promised to her.

"There will be plenty more where that came from," Ryland promised her, pecking her nose sweetly before stepping away from her. He looked toward the direction of the castle, a deep breath being drawn in through his nose as he looked back at her.

"See you on the other side," Ryland chuckled before shooting her a wink and jogging off toward the castle.

Violet watched him go, unable to help but feel a sinking feeling develop in her chest. She tried to shake it off, knowing that she needed to believe in them and the plan. They had gone over the plan numerous times, even discussing back up options if something fell through. They had transportation to get them and the gold out of the Kingdom. They were as prepared as they could possibly be.

After waiting behind the house for a little while, giving Ryland time to get to the castle to prepare the distraction, Violet set off toward the bridge, pulling the hood of her coat up over her head. She felt her knapsack bounce against her back as she walked through the quiet Kingdom, the sunrise glowing bright orange and blue. It was a sight to admire, but she would prefer to admire the gold room once again.

Following her usual path over the bridge and to the side of the iron gates where her spot to get in was, Violet pitched multiple looks over her shoulder, making sure that she wasn't being watched or followed. Luckily, she hadn't seen anyone around really since most were still asleep or in their quarters eating breakfast or getting ready for the day. She slipped through the gap in the gate and then stopped at the side door, wondering if the distraction had been set off yet or not. There was really only one way to find out, prompting her to open the door and slip inside.

Silence greeted her at first as she crept toward the hallway, her shoulder brushing the wall as she kept close to it. She listened closely as she crouched down, trying to hear any noise that sounded throughout the dense and dim castle.

"There's a fire in the north tower!"

"Fire! Fire!"

A smile gradually crossed her face as she heard the commotion. Their planned distraction was for Ryland to sneak into the north tower, which was the weapons storage room, and set fire to it. It sounded like he was successful, and she hoped that he got out safe and was making his way to her location. Since he was a bounty hunter and had been in and out of the castle to talk with the guards and royal family, he was even more aware of the castle's layout than her.

Once the guards that stood in front of the gold room darted past her to head toward the north tower to help, she headed to the room that she had discovered last time that had all of the posters and rolling carts. She needed to borrow a cart, prompting her to sneak in and wheel one out toward the gold room. Now, she could carry a lot more gold out of the room.

Once she got to the door of the gold room, she tried the door handle, which wouldn't budge, making a flush of panic rush through her. One of the guards had the key, and they had all run off. She groaned, trying to focus enough to figure out what to do next. She glanced around for any sort of help, her eyes catching onto a stone torch mounted on a stand on the wall. She reached up and hoisted it off of the stand, grunting at how heavy it was, her breath coming out sharply to blow out the flame before it burnt her.

Violet carried the torch over toward the door handle, her hands gripping the base to lift it like an axe. She swung down at the door handle, slamming the end of the torch against it, a sharp pang sounding from the impact. She checked the door handle to see it hardly hanging on, prompting her to slam the torch down against it again to knock it clear off of the door. She pressed her hand against the door, feeling it give and swing open.

With a relieved sigh, Violet rushed into the room before reaching into her knapsack to pull out a few empty bags that she had packed. She started shoveling gold coins into the bags hurriedly, knowing that she only had so much time before the guards put out the fire and came back. She hauled one full bag of gold coins onto the wooden cart before turning to fill up the other, her hands shaking a degree. Everything was going fine so far, but she was worried that something would happen to change that soon.

Once she finished filling the last bag full of gold coins to the very brim, Violet threw the bag onto the cart just as she heard footsteps approach the door. She drew her knife hurriedly, readying herself for the guards to burst through the door. Instead, Ryland rushed into the room, a few scratches littering his face, along with a busted lip.

"Are you okay?" Violet immediately asked, rushing over to him to cup his face and check him over.

"I'm okay, but we need to leave soon," Ryland told her, gripping her hands gently before moving to grab the cart's handle. He pushed it out of the gold room, gripping the handle tightly to guide the cart toward the side door.

"Where do we go?" Violet asked, only knowing that transportation would be waiting for them. She had entrusted the escape part of the plan to Ryland.

"The bridge," Ryland told her, waiting for her to open the side door before pushing the cart outside of the castle. He hurried his pace, turning the cart around so that he could pull it and drag it toward the bridge within the iron gates.

Violet jogged alongside him, glancing every which way for people as they moved. They were so close to escaping, the excitement shuddering her very bones. She looked ahead toward the bridge, seeing a stagecoach with a driver and two horses sitting there.

"Spared no expense, huh?" She commented as they approached the bridge, running alongside the moat.

"I promised him a cut of our gold," Ryland panted as he shoved open the gate doors and hauled the cart onto the bridge, dragging it toward the stagecoach. Once they reached it, he opened the door to the coach and started to throw the bags of gold inside.

Violet turned her head to see the King outside of the front of the castle with a group of guards, smoke continuing to pour from the window of the north tower. She saw the King point toward them as they approached the bridge, the guards immediately rushing toward Violet and Ryland.

"We've got company," Violet warned Ryland as the guards got closer and closer.

"Go!" Ryland shouted to the driver, signaling for him to start taking off. He turned to Violet, reaching out to grab her hand.

"Get in!" He told her, guiding her into the open door of the coach as it started to move.

Violet threw herself onto the seat, pushing the bags of gold to the side before reaching out to Ryland.

"Come on!" She called to him, knowing that the guards had to be close to catching them. She felt his fingers brush hers as he started to pull himself up toward the door of the coach. At the last second, his eyes widened, and he slipped away to fall onto the bridge, a guard's hand wrapped around his ankle.

Violet cried out in shock as she scrambled to peer out of the stagecoach as it rolled away from Ryland, who struggled against a few guards that where grabbing at him. Panic struck her, nearly freezing her up, but she knew what she had to do.

"Keep going until you hit the main road!" Violet shouted to the driver before jumping out of the stagecoach, her feet slamming against the surface of the bridge before she ran across it to rush to Ryland's aid.

Chapter Nineteen

A KING TO
FIGHT FOR

"Kill them! Kill them both!" The King shouted, his round face reddening. His gold crown was lopsided on his bald head, while his red robe hugged his stout body tightly. He looked naturally angry with narrowed eyes and creases in his forehead, making him seem threatening and ferocious.

Violet drew her knife, immediately throwing it so that it pierced the chest of one of the guards beating down on Ryland, who was pinned down on the ground by three other guards. She ran forward to push the guard over and off of Ryland, her hand gripping the handle of her knife to pull it from his body. She ducked under a swing from one of the other guards, her knee thrusting up to slam against his stomach.

"What are you doing? Kill her, you morons!" The King shouted, stomping his foot against the bridge, his voice already sounding strained from yelling so harshly.

Ryland managed to grab his knife as he endured hit after hit, his arm swinging up to slice the cheek of one of the guards. He fought his way back to his feet, struggling to remain steady as he dodged hits and tried to land some of his own as he still felt dazed and hurt.

Violet glanced at Ryland worriedly, noting how hurt and exhausted he seemed. She shifted her stance closer to him, watching his back as she faced off with a guard. She jabbed at his hand with her knife, keeping him from drawing his short sword. She didn't want to be involved in a blades battle.

The guard facing Violet swung his fist at her head, catching her temple and knocking her off balance.

Violet stumbled along the bridge, scraping her knees as she tried to find her balance again. She threw herself out of the way of a hefty kick, rolling across the bridge before pushing herself to her feet. She felt herself grow tired, her body aching from the hits that she had endured. She twirled her knife in her hand, gripping the blade tight before slashing down at the guard's leg, cutting him from his thigh to his knee to make him stumble and limp.

Ryland found himself overwhelmed by two guards, who hit him from both sides until he fell to the ground again. A groan of pain left him, his hand reaching over to grasp his stomach, trying to protect himself as they kicked at him roughly.

Violet glanced over her shoulder at Ryland, panic thundering through her as she watched the guards attack him with sheer brutality. She moved to rush to him and help him, but the guard she faced off with grabbed her hair and yanked her back. A hiss of pain left her through gritted teeth as he tossed her to the ground roughly near the edge of the bridge, which had no railing, her palms scraping the surface of the bridge painfully as her knife skittered a foot away from her.

"That's it! End them!" The King laughed out, clasping his hands together victoriously as he watched from a few feet away.

The guard hovered over Violet, flipping her onto her back so that he could drive a hit against her stomach, knocking the breath from her. He landed blow after blow, weakening her hit by hit.

Violet threw her hands up, trying to protect herself as much as she could, but the guard was built and strong without harboring any sort of mercy for her. She kicked out a foot when she could, trying to catch the guard in the stomach, but he deflected her hits, having the upper hand.

"Show them what happens when they rival against the royal family!" The King growled out, watching Violet through narrowed eyes as he stood near the edge of the bridge close to her.

Violet had never seen so much hate and greed in someone's eyes, anger flaring through her. The royal family did not get to win. They did not get to take everything that she loved from her. If no one else was going to keep them in check, then she would have to do that herself. Ryland's cries of pain thundered in her head, only fueling the anger that burned through her. She wouldn't lose another person that she loved. She couldn't bear that.

Violet dropped her hands from her face, switching from the defensive to the offensive before the guard could properly react. She drove her fist up, catching him in the nose and breaking it. As he grasped at it in pain, she drove her foot up to kick him off, making the guard stumble away from her, finally freeing her from being pinned to the bridge.

As quickly as she could, Violet rolled toward her knife near the center of the bridge, her hand snatching up its handle. She whipped around, her eyes landing on the King, and then threw the knife with every ounce of force that she had in her body. It was a move halfway thought out, but she didn't regret the sight of the blade burying itself in the King's chest.

The guards beating on Ryland froze, staring at the King in shock as he stumbled backwards, his hand grabbing at the knife clumsily before he toppled over the edge of the bridge and fell down toward the moat below.

Violet stared at the space that the King had just stood in with a shocked look, hardly believing that had just happened. Every ounce of pain and anger that she had harbored over the years toward the royal family had been released in that one throw. It felt like countless pounds of weight had been lifted from her shoulders at last, but the fight wasn't over just yet. She whipped around to face the two guards hovering over Ryland, her eyes narrowing.

Ryland snapped out of his shocked gaze to throw the hardest punch that he could muster at the closest guard, only able to daze the guard momentarily.

Violet took over, shoving one guard into the other to knock them both down as they tripped over Ryland and each other. She grabbed Ryland's knife off of the ground and endured a few hits to deal a few cuts, sending the guards scrambling off of the bridge and away from her. She supposed that they realized that there wasn't really a King to fight for right then.

"We did it," Ryland breathed out from the ground, his breath coming out shakily and painfully as he grasped his torso.

"Almost. We have to get out of here first," Violet reminded him, knowing that they needed to hurry out of the Kingdom to get to the stagecoach that was waiting for them outside of the main gates. She leaned down to help Ryland off of the bridge carefully, throwing his arm over her shoulders. Her body rang with pain, but she pushed through, knowing that they were so close.

"I've got you. I've got you," she breathed out, holding him tightly as they shuffled across the bridge as quickly as they could in their hurt states. She heard him pant and wheeze in pain, coaxing a frown onto her face.

"You killed the King," Ryland breathed out, turning to gaze at her in surprise.

"I wasn't planning on it … but he's never going to stop. He's made his people suffer if he's not killing them for no reason. Someone needed to do it," Violet sighed out, not liking the idea of taking another human life, but the King was hardly human. He was a monster in the body of a human, and monsters deserved to be taken down. She couldn't think of a better way to help the people of the Kingdom, who cowered under his iron fist.

"You're right. He was the worst person I ever met," Ryland muttered, having a personal vendetta against the King. He hopped down from the bridge with a grunt, leaning into her side as they traveled down the road through town to head toward the front gates.

Once they made it through the gates and saw the stagecoach waiting for them, Violet nearly collapsed as relief flooded through her. She willed herself forward for the last few feet until they reached the coach, her hand reaching forward to throw open the door. She crawled inside before reaching out to grab Ryland's hand to pull him inside with her.

Ryland shut the door behind him, falling back against the seat with a sigh.

"Alright, take us to Riverwood," Ryland told the driver before turning to Violet with a smile, glad that they had settled on a village to travel to. If they didn't think that they would fit in, they could always try another. Their next adventure was finding their new home, one that they could be happy in and find fulfillment in.

"Are you okay? You took a beating," Violet asked him, giving him a concerned look. He was bloodied, bruises being promised for the next day, but at least he was still breathing. For a moment there, she had been sure that they were goners, but they fought their way through like they always did.

"I'm fine now. Then, no," Ryland laughed out softly, trying not to chuckle too hard to make his torso hurt. He gingerly placed his arm around Violet's shoulders, pulling her to his side as he glanced over at the two bags full of gold coins.

"We did good. Gram would be proud of you," Ryland told her before pressing a gentle kiss to her temple.

Violet smiled warmly and nodded as she leaned into his touch, hoping that he was right. She had fought hard, putting her life on the line and taking risks. She had never felt so scared in her life, but she also had never felt so alive. During the fight for life, she was the furthest from death, and it was an addicting feeling. However, she wouldn't mind taking a break from fighting for her life for awhile. She had done plenty of it during the last week, and she had someone that she wanted to stay alive for.

"I'm proud of us," Violet murmured, meaning each word with every fiber of her being. They started off so far away from each other, standing on different sides and fighting for different reasons. It was a divide that she never expected to get over, but they became closer in a way that she had never experienced before. He had become a part of her, a detail of her adventure through life. She hadn't ever expected this, but she was glad that it happened.

"I'm glad we made it out alive," Ryland told her with a bright smile before resting the side of his head against hers, letting the soft sway of the coach rock him.

Violet closed her eyes with an agreeing nod, feeling her body grow heavy as the tension started to melt away. It was like finally breathing after being underwater for a long time. The relief filled her to the brim, and peace settled over her. She hoped that it stayed with them for as long as possible. It was ironic for a pair of fighters to desire peace so much, but there had to be a balance in the chaos of their lives. However, she didn't mind a little chaos to keep things fun. What was an adventure without a little risk?

Chapter Twenty

LITTLE FIGHTERS

Six months later

"Watch out! She's going to get you!" The shout rang out through the village's courtyard, echoing off of the cobble streets and timber framed houses. Despite the urgency of the call, the villagers piddling around the streets and the nearby market didn't look up or appear alarmed. To them, it was a normal noise, one that brought more amusement than fear.

"I was watching her!" A boy around the age of twelve groaned as he shifted his wooden sword in his hand. He turned to his teacher, a pouted look adorning his face as his shaggy, black hair nearly fell into his eyes.

Ryland tossed his head back with a laugh, his hand resting on his stomach as it ached from amusement. He shook his head gently at the boy before placing his hand on his shoulder.

"That's okay, Oliver. Just make sure you watch all sides so that she can't sneak up on you," Ryland encouraged him, patting him on the shoulder before gesturing for Oliver to spar against a red-haired girl around his age, who had a wooden sword of her own.

"Don't let your eyes betray you, Isabelle," Violet called to the girl as she stepped up to Ryland's side, a soft breeze blowing against the shoulder-length strands of her blonde hair. She watched them with pride, feeling a distinct thumping in her chest as they used the skills and knowledge that they had been taught. She then looked over at Ryland and smiled, listening to their students engage in a light battle to test and improve their offensive and defensive skills.

"They're learning so quickly," Violet murmured to him, her voice full of warmth. They had worked with the two kids for the past few weeks, and their skills had increased tenfold. They had plenty of other students, ranging from all sorts of different ages, but children were their favorite to teach. Starting them from the ground up and watching them grow along with their skills was a reward all on its own. She wished that she had teachers like this when she was growing up. Teaching herself had been hard and grueling, nearly leading her to giving up multiple times. She was incredibly glad that she didn't.

"No one is going to dare to try to invade Riverwood," Ryland chuckled as he watched Isabelle sidestep a jab from Oliver. It reminded him of watching Violet fight, which was something they hadn't done in quite a long time. Danger had only threatened them once since they came to Riverwood in the form of bandits. They had fought them off, but it showed Ryland Violet how unprepared the small village was when it came to danger. The town hardly had any sort of defense besides wooden fences around the area. So, they figured out a way to help.

"We've basically trained our own guards. I'm glad the village leader let us open up our practice," Violet told Ryland before calling to Oliver and Isabelle that the lesson was over. After telling them goodbye wistfully and watching them run off down the main road toward their respective houses, Violet led Ryland into their own shared house with a soft sigh.

Ryland kicked off his boots in the small foyer, nudging them up against the wall before following her past the kitchen and into the main room of the house that had a fireplace. It was a house that displayed both of their personalities with all sorts of herbs in the kitchen and a weapons room across the hallway from their bedroom. They had souvenirs placed all over the house from their various adventures, including interesting rocks, rare gems, and artifacts from roadside vendors.

"I paid Aaron for his horses that we'll take tomorrow," Ryland told her as they moved to sit in front of the fireplace for a few minutes. He drew a pack of matches out of his belt before leaning forward to relight the fire to illuminate the interior of the house, the reflection of the growing flame dancing in the green of his eyes.

"I'm so excited! Where are we going?" Violet asked as she shifted over closer to him, batting her eyelashes in a playful manner. Ryland had been planning a little out of town adventure for them for the past week, but he hadn't given up any hints as to where they were going. She was desperate to know and ready to explore a new place.

"It's supposed to be a surprise," Ryland told her pointedly, an amused smile crossing his face as he watched her lean close with a pout on her face. He pressed his lips to her forehead in response, placing his hand on her knee affectionately.

"Please tell me. Not knowing is torturous," Violet groaned, gripping his hand in hers. She nudged him, prodding him to give in and tell her.

Ryland hummed playfully, pretending to ponder on her words. Eventually, he sighed in defeat and turned to her with a smile.

"There are springs half a day's ride away from here. The water is the bluest that you'll ever see, and it's the perfect temperature for a swim," Ryland described the place to her, having been recommended the place by a local in the village.

The people in Riverwood had proved to be really warm and welcoming, helping them settle into a vacant house and start up their combat training business. The village was grateful to have some level of protection, and it further convinced Ryland and Violet to choose this village as the place to settle down in. It helped that it was far away from the Kingdom as well.

"Springs? That sounds perfect!" Violet exclaimed, having never visited any before. She pressed a grateful kiss to his cheek, knowing that he had been working hard getting everything set up for tomorrow. As they got settled over the past six months, they had grown even closer, spending their days and nights together. They talked about everything, trained together, went into business together, and even occasionally fished together in a nearby lake. However, they also had a favorite activity to share together.

"Let's go sit on the hills," Violet told him as she stood up, reaching down to grab his hand and tug him along with her. She knew that they were supposed to be resting after their training session, but the sky was so blue, and it felt so warm today. They couldn't possibly keep themselves cooped up inside when there was such a beautiful view to experience.

Once Violet led Ryland out of their house and down the road toward the village's exit, she gazed around at her surroundings.

"Good afternoon!" An older man called to them from across the road, lifting his hand in a wave as he tended to his garden in front of his house.

"Hi, Mr. Neal!" Violet greeted him, waving back before continuing on her way. Their neighbors were kind and accommodating. Most of the children in the village were enrolled in their combat training. They had organized a militia to help defend the village if it ever got attacked. So many things had fallen into place when they arrived in Riverwood, like their luck did a complete turn from what it was back in the Kingdom. It had felt like she couldn't catch a break there.

"David is going to have a few more wooden swords made for us in a couple of days," Ryland told her with an excited smile. David was the village's carpenter, and he appreciated their service to the town so much that he regularly provided them with the wooden swords that they used for training. In the village, everyone tried to do what they could to help each other.

"He's great. All of these people are great. I feel like we've been welcomed into a new family," Violet replied, meaning her words. After everything that had happened with Gram and the fight at the Kingdom, Ryland had been a huge help to her, making sure that she stayed sane through the emotional aftermath. However, she did suffer a gap in her life that the village helped fill. They treated her like family, took care of her like she was a daughter or a granddaughter. It helped soothe the pain of losing her last family member a little.

"We ended up in the right place," Ryland agreed, lifting her hand to kiss her knuckles adoringly as they walked at each other's sides.

Violet blushed, still feeling bashful over actions like that. She had only fallen deeper and deeper in love with him as the days went on, especially when they did things together, like adventuring or even shopping for food together in the village's market. Those small moments carried nearly as much weight as the big ones.

After walking out of the village for a few minutes, rolling green hills greeted them, little, white flowers nestled in the grass. They made their way to the top of one of them, sitting on the curve and looking out at the village as they leaned their shoulders against each other. The breeze ruffled through their hair, ghosting over their skin.

"I can't believe we actually made it … through everything … the forest, the guards, the King, the road here," Ryland breathed out in awe as he looked out, a proud look adorning his face.

Violet smiled and nodded her agreement, hardly able to believe it either. The odds hadn't exactly been in their favorite at the start of it all. They faced so many obstacles, ones that nearly killed them and split them apart. Them being able to survive was a miracle in some instances, but it was mostly all due to their teamwork. They played off of each other's strengths and weaknesses, picking up the slack when one of them fell. Most importantly, they never ever abandoned each other, always remaining at each other's sides no matter how tough things got, and they got especially tough at some points.

"When it comes to danger, I would bet all of my gold on us every single time," she admitted with a little laugh, glancing away from the village toward him. They still had a good amount of gold to their name from the raid at the Kingdom, including more that they had earned from their business. However, they made it a point to invest back into the village, helping people in need and buying local goods and services. If the village treated them like family, they would treat the village the exact same way.

"Gambling girl, eh?" Ryland teased her, nudging her with his shoulder before tossing his arm over her shoulders and drawing her close to his side.

"I think the odds are in my favor this time," Violet pointed out, gesturing to the space around them. They had finally reached the paradise that they strived for, and peace surrounded them on all sides. Threats were few and far between, but they still kept each other on their toes in case things took a dangerous turn.

Ryland held her gaze for a few deep moments, a look of pure adoration filling his face.

"I love you. You know that, right?" Ryland murmured.

Violet felt a hitch in her breath at his words, her heart rate immediately etching up in response as she nodded. She did know that he loved her because he showed it in so many ways. He kept her safe, motivated her, made sure that she was comfortable, and made her happy. He went through more lengths to make her feel safe and happy than anyone else had done for her before.

"I love you too. I was scared of feeling this way at first because … I've never felt these feelings before, but I trust you. That means as much as love to me," Violet told him, feeling his thumb rub soft circles against her upper arm beneath the black fabric of her short-sleeve shirt. Trust meant a lot to her, especially since there weren't many people in her life that she had trusted before coming to the village. Of course, it had taken some time to warm up to

Ryland, but after them both saving each other, she soon developed a strong feeling of trust for him, and it had only grown throughout the days.

"You can always trust me because I'm always going to be here with you," Ryland promised her, lifting his other hand up to caress her cheek. He shared a warm smile with her before drawing her lips to his, his eyes closing at the soft touch.

Violet sank down into the feeling, wanting the warmth to last forever. Every motion and touch felt like countless moments with him, and she wanted to maintain their eternity. She pressed her lips against his one more time before pulling away from him with a soft laugh.

"I don't know how things could get even better," she told him honestly, not sure of what was next for them. They had been so focused on getting settled that they hadn't really looked ahead into their future together. There were a lot of options and a lot to consider, but they hadn't taken the time to discuss those choices with each other.

"It's been nice teaching those kids. You're really great with them," Ryland commented, a small smile quirking up on his lips. There seemed to be hidden weight behind his words, and Violet soon caught on.

A deep blush flamed up on Violet's cheeks as she gazed down at the ground bashfully. She loved helping the kids learn. They took to her and Ryland well, always excited to go to their lessons. It even made her a bit sad when they had to leave, and she couldn't deny that she felt something fluttering in her chest when she watched Ryland interact with them. He was a natural.

"We've taught them to be fighters," Violet laughed softly, leaning her head against Ryland's shoulder and gazing up at him lovingly, like stars filled her blue eyes.

"We could raise little fighters of our own," Ryland pointed out, lifting his eyebrows a bit as he grinned at her. He looked hopeful and happy, a light shine adorning his eyes.

Violet felt herself automatically nodding, excitement rushing through her as she hugged him happily. They both had faced major misfortunes when it came to family. They could repair what had broken them, ensuring that their children had the best childhood with parents that were around. Violet knew that her parents couldn't help what happened to them, but she would do everything in her power to make sure that she and Ryland were around for their children.

"Yes, of course! We'll be a family to not mess with," Violet laughed out, knowing they would be tough and fierce, protecting each other no matter what. She wished that Gram would be around to see her great grandchildren, but Violet would tell her children stories about the witch that raised her. She would tell them about how their parents met and fought for each other every minute. She would tell them that they were loved and that they would never be left behind. No matter what, they would make it through as long as they all had each other.